THE TRAIN NOW DEPARTING

G·K
Hall
&Cº

Also by Martha Grimes
in Large Print:

RICHARD JURY NOVELS
The Man with a Load of Mischief
The Old Fox Deceived
The Anodyne Necklace
The Dirty Duck
Jerusalem Inn
Help the Poor Struggler
The Deer Leap
I Am the Only Running Footman
The Five Bells and Bladebone
The Old Silent
The Stargazey
The Lamorna Wink

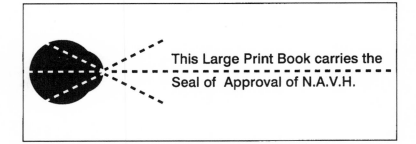

This Large Print Book carries the
Seal of Approval of N.A.V.H.

MARTHA GRIMES

THE TRAIN NOW DEPARTING

TWO NOVELLAS

G.K. Hall & Co. • Thorndike, Maine

Published in 2000 by arrangement with Viking Penguin, a division of Penguin Putnam, Inc.

G.K. Hall Large Print Core Series.

The text of this Large Print edition is unabridged.
Other aspects of the book may vary from the original edition.

Set in 16 pt. Plantin by Susan Guthrie.

Printed in the United States on permanent paper.

Library of Congress Cataloging-in-Publication Data

Grimes, Martha.
    The train now departing : two novellas / Martha Grimes.
        p.   cm.
    Contents: The train now departing — When the mousetrap closes.
    ISBN 0-7838-9071-0 (lg. print : hc : alk. paper)
        1. Single women — Fiction. 2. Large type books. I. Title.
    PS3557.R48998 T73 2000b
        813'.54—dc21   00-036982

CONTENTS

THE TRAIN NOW DEPARTING

9

WHEN *THE MOUSETRAP* CLOSES

145

THE TRAIN
NOW
DEPARTING

ONE

She had been speaking of the railway station, and he, as usual, had abandoned any pretense of listening, his attention solidly fixed upon his food, his fork aimed as if he were waging war on his lamb chops. The concentration with which he attacked his plate left no room for "banter" (as he referred to most of her conversation). But were she to accuse him of not listening, he would claim he certainly had been, to every word, and would then go into one of his elaborately mocking displays by setting down his knife and fork and fixing her with a wide-eyed stare, as if to say, There, is that what you want? thus making her appear demanding and contentious.

It was one of their long late-afternoon lunches, and she wondered why they continued to have them, since they annoyed each other so much. He was as usual eating something heavy, explaining that it would also serve as dinner. That way, he would not have to bother going out again later on. The main reason he liked late lunches, he told her, was because of his writing schedule; he liked to start around nine and continue on through the early afternoon. He could never write after a meal, he said, so he put off the meal until three or four.

She had ordered a salad of mixed greens. The restaurant was French and so the menu didn't call it that; its description of the salad was complicated and euphemistic. She wondered how they managed to catch greens at the "baby" stage; did greens also have an adolescence, an adulthood? But however the menu tried to enrich it, the salad was still mixed greens.

As an appetizer, he had ordered mussels to which a number of things had been done, including sautéing and saucing up. She didn't know one did such things to mussels. She had ordered tomato juice. Without looking up from his dish of mussels, he had asked her how her tomato juice was, as if anything really interesting could be done with tomato juice. The question *How is this?* or *How was that?* — repeated at every lunch — was one of his few ready contributions to the conversation. It was for him an obligatory question, one which demonstrated his interest in her enjoyment. He always asked it of one dish or another, often several times during the course of a meal, thereby discharging his conversational debt.

The waiter came with the wine, and he and the waiter discussed the year and the vineyard, speaking in rapid-fire French. After the waiter poured a thimbleful for tasting, it was pronounced good or very good (*"Bon, bon"*). The label told her it was a Hermitage, one of the reds he was so fond of. He always chose well and, in choosing well, spent a great amount of money. This was his favorite restaurant because of its wine list. He had spent months in Burgundy, in Meursault, Chablis, and Puligny-Montrachet, but he did not talk about the trip as such: the customs, the people, the lie of the land. Or, to be more precise, he *did* speak of the lie of the land insofar as it involved the slopes of the vineyards, how a few feet might separate a good wine from a great.

But he approached such subjects as if she knew all about them, yet she knew nothing at all about them. Why he assumed she was conversant with such topics as that particular vineyard which produced a *grand cru,* its exposure to sun and cold, its particular soil — this she simply couldn't imagine, since he so often accused her of bantering and foolishness. But there he had been, at a previous lunch and another table, going on about Puligny, the source of his beloved Montrachet, going on as if she'd lived in the village herself. He had talked about Chablis — "You know those vineyards that produce the best Chardonnay grapes?" — and she had interrupted to assure him she had never been anywhere near Chablis, never been to Burgundy, never to *France;* didn't he know that? She knew he knew it; still, he paid no attention. And when she thought surely she could lead him around to describing the villages and the countryside he

11

would just shrug and say something about his rental car breaking down or the poor condition of the roads.

It was not that he did not talk, it was that he went through *bouts* of talking, words like gusts of wind, blowing in, stirring up currents, and troubling the air around them for a few moments. The brief exchange with the waiter about the Crozes-Hermitage was like this. In the course of lunching with him at many different restaurants, she had discovered that he was fluent in French, Italian, Spanish, and probably German, as he'd spent a good deal of time in Cologne, too. But she would not find out until they went to a German restaurant. When she had expressed surprise at his astonishing fluency in these languages, he had shrugged and said, "Well, one picks them up."

Their main course came and another swift exchange in French (the waiter happy he could "banter" in his own language). Now that their entrées had come, she could expect all conversation to be suspended while they ate. In place of conversation, after a certain amount of time and silence pressed upon them, he would ask her the obligatory question. Since she was having salad, he would ask about that.

Her main course — the salad — did not charm her; the greens were greens, even if they had been plucked in their infancy, and the dressing was too sharp, too vinegary. It made no difference to her; she hadn't been hungry. She would have preferred to be in the station café, eating the grilled-cheese sandwich she usually ordered. The station was one of those handsome nineteenth-century railway stations, and unusual in that it had been one of those in which the agents and their families had lived at the turn of the century. It fascinated her to think that part of it had been occupied by a family once. It was near her own large house, of that same Victorian period. She had lived all her life in this house. Her family had been small, very small, and were now all dead; not only her father and her mother, all of them — the few aunts and uncles, the tiny sprinkling of cousins. She wondered how that could be. It was almost as if a passenger car on a train carrying everyone together had disappeared. *Where be your gibes now? your gambols? your songs? your flashes of merriment?* She caught her breath. Such fragments often overtook her, coming so swiftly they made her wince.

"How's your salad?"

She was not prepared for the question this time, and she felt tears well in the corners of her eyes. Tears of sadness and also of frustration. She wanted to slap him. At the very least, she would like to say, Awful, it's awful, but this would only have cued him to disregard her or contradict her: Looks perfectly all right to me. Something like that. "Fine" is what she said, and he continued eating his chops, probably without hearing the answer, certainly without caring about it.

Over cocktails, she had been trying to get him to talk about Zimbabwe. But he had, as she knew he would, answered in monosyllables. She had realized soon after they met that to try and draw him out about his trips was bound to end in failure, for he would not be drawn. He would drop hints only of the exoticism of what he had seen. As today, between the end of his first course of mussels and the beginning of his lamb, he had slipped into the silence the information that there were fish in the Amazon capable of swallowing cows. She waited for him to explain this brilliant fact, perfectly aware that he wouldn't. He went on eating his lamb.

He managed to travel to these places without affect (except, perhaps, for Burgundy), dropping astounding bits of information into the silences that made up the large part of their meals together, as if he were reporting on the weather outside. It was so peculiar. Had he been a charming person, this might have been the charmingly innocent act of a schoolboy. Only he wasn't charming. And he hadn't a sense of what they called "childlike wonder." He seemed to assume that everyone knew, for instance, about Quetzalcoatl, the plumed serpent; or Silbaco, the nightjar that haunts the forests of the Amazon. And he would speak of these things without enlarging upon them. *That* was what, above all, exasperated her beyond saying. Well, what good did it do to *say?* He merely grunted or shrugged or suggested she was being *trying* or overly literal.

14

It was not that he was keeping these trips secret, quite the contrary: he talked like a man with no secrets to hide. When she really got irritated with him, she could question him quite mercilessly and take a perverse pleasure in his side-stepping, evading, and shooting down her questions, dropping them like dead birds on the table.

They had had to build a raft to take them up the Yata River.

"Of what? How did you build it?"

"Balsa and vines." He shrugged. Anyone could do it.

"Is — was — the river pretty?"

"No. Where's the damned waiter?"

So the river she would have to picture on her own. Brown and sinuous, islands of floating greenery, pink wading birds, luxuriant trees growing from the water. Eyes flashing through the dark vegetation. . . . She sighed. All she knew about jungles she supposed she'd got from Joseph Conrad.

"What's wrong? Why are you glooming away?" he asked.

"I'm not glooming. I'm merely trying to picture the river."

"What river?"

She dropped her head, sipped her coffee, recalling that he had taken a train, but from where to where she couldn't remember. He had said only that it was hot, crowded, dreadful. He would not expand upon that, though to her it sounded as if it must surely have been colorful, in spite of the discomfort. "Wasn't it colorful?"

"Not particularly." He had found the waiter. More bread, more wine.

It was his mention of the train that made her think of their own railway station — how uninhabited it always seemed, how deserted.

As a child she remembered going to meet the train with her mother, standing on the platform in a cloud of steam, watching the conductor drop down the yellow step for passengers descending, and assisting the ladies with an old-world courtly manner. The steam settling like fog or ground mist, the snow a bright unbroken crust that lay around the station, reflecting back the gold light inside, and a frill of snow along each window ledge like the whipped-cream piping on a cake or a flourish of lace on a dress.

She mentioned it to him — not the memory of her childhood but the train station itself, how deserted it had always seemed. "It's like a ghost station. Ghost trains steaming through a ghost station."

"*Diesel*-ing through, you mean." He smiled slyly. He knew she liked the image of the ghost train and so decided to demolish it. Still smiling, he continued eating.

"You accuse me of being literal, but it's you who are. I've never known a writer to be so literal." She flushed with both anger and embarrassment, as if caught out in the middle of a childish fantasy.

16

"You've never known a writer *at all*, other than myself."

"Me," she said. "Other than *me*." That was a weak refutation, merely correcting his grammar. She hurried on. "Didn't you have fun watching the steam trains when you were young? They seemed to have so much more . . . authority than the ones we have now." There was no point in bringing up his childhood, she knew, for he never reminisced. Whereas, that was what she did mostly and well.

"If you like them so much, you should go to Zimbabwe," he said.

She blinked at this astonishing irrelevancy. "Why in heaven's name Zimbabwe?"

"The trains all run on steam there. It's the coal, you see. Country's loaded with coal."

Missing the point completely. He usually did. She wondered if missing it weren't deliberate.

He had returned from Zimbabwe, and it was as if he'd taken a walk around the corner for a newspaper. He traveled a good six months out of the year, and though he avoided talking about his travels (that is, beyond the startling comment or two), he wrote about them, and that, he must have supposed, was enough. He was a travel writer. She had read bits and pieces of his books because of their lunches together and because she knew him. She felt she must. She did not dislike his books; she was quite astounded that events were so colorfully reported. But she'd rather not read about travel. Travel writing made her uncomfortable; she did not know why. Perhaps because she felt she should travel herself but grew anxious merely thinking about it. Still, she had to give him credit for not answering her questions with Read my book, it's all in my book. He did not refer to his books as sources. Indeed, he did not refer to his books at all. At first she thought this might stem from sheer indifference. He did not seem to care about the books, except by way of complaining about the publishing business, how inept "those people" were.

She sipped her wine and thought it tasted flinty. It was extremely dry. "It's the anonymity of a train ride I like."

"You never go anywhere, so how do you know?" He was separating the meat from the bone of his third chop, careful as a surgeon. They were quite small, the chops. But "baby lamb" was obviously redundant.

She went on. "It's eerie. As if the self were in some kind of limbo."

He was chewing and looking at her, but she doubted he was listening. Or, if listening, comprehending. Often, when he looked up from his food, he would fix her with the glazed look of a child confronted with an irritated parent, seeming to hear but not hearing. Tuning out. There but not there.

The waiter came to replenish their water and wine. "*Our* station — why is it so empty nearly all of the time?" This was not what she meant. She meant, Why does it make me *feel* empty, as if I were as devoid of experience as one of the waiting-room benches or one of the loosened panes rattling in the wind? She would sit on one of these benches, against a wall painted a dull cream, woodwork a varnished brown, colors she would have liked to think were chosen because they wouldn't agitate one's mind. The station and the platform were always spotlessly clean. There was a dog, too, a Labrador mixed with other breeds, its coat brown and slightly shiny like the woodwork. She supposed it belonged to the stationmaster. The dog was well fed and friendly and sometimes came to sit beside her. And there was, of course, the lunchroom, the café. It was the area that once must have served as the living quarters for the family. The mother might even have cooked in the café's tiny kitchen. She was at a loss to understand how it took in enough business to keep going. Many times she had been the only customer. The station had the air of a place deserted, fled from. The vacant waiting room, the lost property counter with its double door shut and locked, the abandoned ticket window, its tan blind pulled down: CLOSED. All of this was a landscape of sorts that she could relate to.

During these reflections, she had barely noticed the waiter had been and gone, removing the plates, taking her half-eaten salad away. She hadn't wanted it, had found it dull. Now the waiter had returned with the dessert: sorbet for her and, for him, a complicated confection of ivory-colored mousse in a *sauce cassis,* crowned with nuts and other adornments.

"Well," he said, "you've certainly been sitting there glooming away." There was the sly smile again.

Silence on his part was meant to indicate he was not interested in idle chatter; on her part, silence meant moodiness, an uneven, quixotic temperament. It made her smile to think this, for she considered her temperament to be quite bland, smooth and white like the mousse. "I was just picturing our station. Just wondering if anyone buys tickets anymore. The window's always closed, it seems."

Having forced her into saying something, he now ignored what she said and spooned into a rather unappetizing puddle of purple sauce. What was the name of it in French? *La mousse en cassis?* Something involved, like the dessert itself.

"La salle des pas perdus."

She was startled. "What?" Occasionally he would produce a comment of eerie relevance, even though she had been so sure he hadn't been listening.

"It's how the French used to refer to the hall of ticket windows. The booking hall, I suppose they called it. *La salle des pas perdus.* The place of lost footsteps."

Her spoon hung in midair, frozen in time.

"How's your sorbet?" he asked.

20

TWO

The place of lost footsteps.

She thought of that now, sitting in the station café eating a wedge of berry pie, forgetting whether she'd asked the waitress for blueberry or boysenberry. Steam rose from the café's surfaces, from the grill and the Pyrex coffeemakers, and condensed on the windows. The café was empty except for her and the waitress and, back in the small kitchen, the cook. The waitress stood smoking and looking out of the window that faced the platform and the tracks. Occasionally she rubbed away a circle of steam with her forearm, pulling down the sleeve of her sweater to do it. There was nothing to see except the difference between inside and outside.

She went on eating the pie, which was not very appealing because it was cold and the crust a little clammy. The waitress had offered to heat it up for her in the microwave oven, but she had said, No, it was fine the way it was. It tasted more like the kind of pie you would expect to get in a railway café — and that was what it was called: RAILWAY CAFÉ was written on the glass of the door that opened onto the platform. She preferred eating something that gave her a sense of where she was, a sense of place. One would not expect to get a piece of hot pie in such a place. Not that it wasn't good; it was, despite the crust.

When she finished the pie, she too reached over to the window by her table and wiped a circle of mist away to look out. It was raining again, not hard, just a steady drizzle. When it was raining, she especially enjoyed being inside the café. Nicer yet if this café had been that railway café or pub in the film — what was it? — *Brief Encounter*, that was it. The doctor took a cinder out of the woman's eye in the café of a railway station. It was in Britain, where they were called *station-buffets*. Sometimes *caffs*. No, a *caff* was more general; it didn't have to be part of a station. But that station-buffet must have seemed a haven to them right after they met, and a hell of memories when they knew they couldn't meet again.

She studied the crumbs on her plate and looked around the empty café, thinking how fortunate they were to have one in their station and how unusual this was. For a while she sat and fantasized about the families that used to live here, here in the room that was now the café. It was large enough to have been at least three smaller rooms, and the present kitchen and bath could have been just where they were now. What would it have been like to live this close to the trains? She could almost feel the floorboards shudder under her feet.

Was the café (she wondered) subsidized by the town, paid for out of town taxes as a public amenity? Was that how it managed? If that was the case, she was glad her tax dollar was going toward something useful.

Her cup was drained now and she thought she would like more coffee but didn't want to disturb the waitress, still standing at the end of the counter, now with a fresh cigarette. And, besides, she knew she would want to come back later for coffee. Right now she would walk up and down the platform, look at the mail sacks, and later watch them being loaded. (She had no idea that the people around here were such letter writers!) She could look at the posters in the waiting room, which never changed, and the notices posted on the bulletin board outside by the door. Train schedules were posted there, along with notifications of changes or delays. Then, back here for another cup of coffee.

Her stomach felt uncomfortable, heavy from the cold pie. But that was all right; she had known it would. It was part of its café identity.

"You spend too much time there," her writer friend had gone on to say when she had mentioned the sadness trains aroused in her. He was talking about the station while eating a salad whose complex arrangement seemed more a problem in geometry than a plate of food. This had been another week after his return from the

23

Amazon, and it took place in a restaurant he frequently patronized. She did not like it, all of its glass and greenery. Potted palms, spider plants with low-hanging tendrils that sometimes brushed her cheek. She had asked him if the restaurant reminded him somehow of the Amazon rain forest.

"Jungle," he said, irritably.

She was always irritating him, so that made her smile. "Jungle?"

"*Rain forest* is a euphemism the conservationists made up. Something to save. Would you want to save a jungle?"

She thought a moment. "I might." Knowing it would irritate him more.

The room had the appearance of frigid cleanliness. She guessed that the kitchen was dirty. The restaurant was also pretentious and had a fancy menu with the offerings in cursive, as though written as freshly as the radicchio had been picked.

His comment about her spending too much time at the station had been made without conviction, without really caring, and without expecting an answer.

So she hadn't answered. She studied his large plate of salad. He was eating the cold duck salad with radicchio and endive and a few other things, including a sprinkle of pine nuts. The salad was fancy, composed. She wished restaurateurs and their chefs would give up looking at salads as if they were paintings or mathematical problems.

The duck breasts had been arranged in a pyramid around the radicchio core and all of it dressed in one of those hard-to-grasp dressings with four or five main ingredients. How could she consider "garlic-apple-Dijon–mustard" as a separate entity? How could she taste it in her mind?

When she looked at the slices of duck breast she thought of the mallards in the pond in the park. When the sun shone down, their colors were neon-bright. To be brought to such ignominy as this, arranged on a salad plate. She looked up at the shadowed ceiling, thinking she had seen a flash of blue-green wing.

The Railway Café would serve a salad of pale green iceberg lettuce, quarters of tomatoes, onion rings. She had never ordered one, but she could visualize it.

He mentioned a recent film that had received good reviews. "Have you seen it?"

"No." She hadn't wanted to.

"Everyone's seen it. Why not?"

"Well, it's meant to be deep. To make you think."

"Yes. What's wrong with that?"

"That sort of film seems — artificial." She wanted to say *pompous* or *pretentious,* but since he had apparently liked it, he would be insulted. Even so, he felt her refusing to see the film reflected on his own taste.

"You can't criticize what you haven't seen."

"Yes, that's true." It wasn't. She simply wanted

to bring this difference of opinion to a swift close before it escalated into argument. She did not mind argument; it could be stimulating. But not with him. His arguments were boring. She smiled again, wondering why they put up with each other.

The place of lost footsteps.

She was standing in the waiting room by the ticket window. The blind was pulled down with closed coldly printed in large letters. But it was always CLOSED; at least it was whenever she looked inside the station. It must be open sometimes; otherwise, where did people buy their tickets?

For a few moments she sat on one of the benches against the wall and imagined huge, busy stations with *booking halls. Les salles.* Salons, she supposed. She pictured the Gare du Nord, Victoria, and Waterloo — stations she'd never seen and so had to imagine their block-long rows of ticket windows, the booking halls. *Les salles.*

Wasn't travel supposed to offer promise? Hope for the future? The going forth, the undertaking of change? Finally letting go the breath you'd been holding? Freedom? Stacks of luggage, hurrying porters. Promise. Purpose. Why then the *lost footsteps?*

She felt there was something here she should be able to grasp immediately, but she couldn't see it. Instead, she saw herself in one of those enormous vaulted stations, moving slowly, like an elderly person, stopping off in one of its cafés, drinking coffee. Looking through a window. *The place of lost footsteps.*

How was it he was able to tell her such things, he who seemed to place so little value on them? How did he know them? It did not seem fitting he should know them.

It did not seem fair.

THREE

He was a writer of travel narratives, and she had, at the beginning of their acquaintance, reasonably expected his conversation would be filled with details of what he had seen and heard and felt in the places he'd been to. These places sounded exotic and romantic: Jaipur, Aix-en-Provence, Beijing, Patmos. The names glowed, throbbed with color. She saw in her mind's eye sunrises in Tahiti, sunsets in the Peloponnese. Dazzling colors.

One of their lunches took place after he'd just got back from Russia. She'd asked, "How was St. Petersburg?" and been astonished that there were really people of whom one could ask such questions. *How was Marrakesh? Did you like Sorrento?* That he was one of these people amazed her.

"Cold," he said. "Cold as marble." He spoke between bites of radicchio, eating a salad with one of those involved dressings. He was excavating for pine nuts. He did not like them. *They tasted like grit, like gravel,* he said. *Like something the hens go scratching in.* "So was Brussels." He

28

found another pine nut, discarded it on his bread plate.

She waited for him to go on about St. Petersburg or even Brussels, but instead he asked her why she was only having coffee. Why hadn't she ordered any lunch?

"I'm not hungry." Which was not true; she simply disliked the food served in this restaurant. It looked like it wasn't meant to be eaten, but merely gazed at and appreciated. Artfully designed, a palette of colors. Jade pea pods, garnet beets. A plate of vegetables like a neon sign. What she wanted was her grilled-cheese sandwich with a slice of tomato inside at the station café. All she knew now of St. Petersburg and Brussels was that they were cold. She tried to imagine them. Snow and ermine in St. Petersburg. That made her sigh. The image was probably suggested by some film she'd seen, possibly *Doctor Zhivago*. And she also pictured that central square called the Grand'Place in Brussels. Flickers of light all around the square like stars in the dark night. She knew this because van Gogh had painted it: the brilliant stars, the lamps saturated with light. Van Gogh had noticed something more than the cold.

"You should eat," he said, as his salad was replaced by a plate of quail and crystal-green asparagus.

The quail were so small and delicate-looking, each wearing those little paper ruffs at the ends of the legs, the plate made her want to weep. And

29

because of that, she smiled instead. A tight smile.

"What's so amusing?" he asked.

"Oh. I was just thinking about St. Petersburg."

"You wouldn't like it." He stabbed his fork into the tiny bird.

She turned away. Then she said, "That large square in Brussels — it must be beautiful."

"You should travel, if travel is so attractive to you."

Of course, he had turned it into a veiled criticism of her sedentary life. She said, "It isn't."

He dropped the travel and said, "You should get out more."

He was always saying this. It was because he didn't care if she did or didn't that he kept saying the same thing. She ignored the remark as she always did and turned her head to look out of the bay window. At its top was a jungle of fern and tangled vines. She noticed the leaves were dusty.

"I saw you in that coffee shop at the station. Why do you go there? It's awful."

"No it isn't." She had told herself many times not to be defensive around him, for it only whetted his appetite for confrontation. Still, she went on. "They make marvelous omelets, the best I've ever eaten." It was true. When she'd tasted the first one, she could hardly believe that such a simple little place, a common café, could make such an omelet. "It's very high and light because the whites are beaten stiff, like a soufflé."

He was shaking and shaking his head.

"You've never eaten there, so how do you know it's awful?" She tried to keep the irritation out of her voice, but couldn't.

He rolled his eyes in a heaven-help-us manner (clearly feeling that the question didn't deserve an answer) and buttered the last of the bread.

She found it irritating that he simply dismissed her question. He could criticize what *he* hadn't experienced, but she could not criticize what she was sure was the underlying falseness of the film he had liked. He would never admit the truth of this, though.

He studied his bread and finally answered her. "Because of what it looks like — a greasy spoon."

She hadn't heard that hackneyed description in years. She persisted, knowing it was fruitless to try to make him concede any point of hers. "Well, you should go there and try an omelet. Then you'd see how good it is." Immediately, she was sorry she'd said this, for she did not want him to go to the Railway Café and find fresh subject for criticism, all the more because he knew it was something she enjoyed. Worse, he might spoil the place. He would leave behind a trail of dust, a spirit dust, perhaps, that would remain after he'd gone. And some of him would then be forever seated at one of the tables, and even if she couldn't see the shape of him, she would be aware that he'd been there, had touched the sugar bowl, had lifted the salt and pepper, plucked out napkins. There would be spiritual fingerprints everywhere.

"I wouldn't be caught dead," he said.

For the hundredth time, she had to ask herself why she kept the friendship alive. Well, she could not cut out everyone, and she had in the last few years allowed other relationships to wither and die. Better ones than this, too. Thus, she told herself she must be extremely careful, that she should hold on to these few people even if they were incapable of really having a conversation — for she always assumed that this occurred only on some level of intimacy. This did not mean confessing or revealing hidden things. That was another level of intimacy.

So she kept on with him, despite his ill humor, his carping, his buried rage. She felt it must be that — genuine rage at some object he had no access to. Dead parents, perhaps. His indifference to her was scarcely more than his indifference to himself. This was perhaps the most peculiar thing — not his indifference to her but to himself. He was not proud or egotistical about what he had done, and he had done some rather dangerous things (she had learned from reading his books). But it was as if he were speaking of somebody else, someone he didn't much care for.

Understanding this didn't matter much, strangely. It was still painful, his disregard of her. Now the Railway Café would offer a subject for fresh criticism, even though he hadn't been in it. He had worn thin the usual topics. How many times had she heard him tell her she should "get out more"?

He used it now to question her conduct. "You spend too much time there."

She sighed. "But why were you there? Where were you buying a ticket to?"

He mentioned the city, unhappy with it even though it was merely a point of departure for the greater trip. "It's where I get the ship for Polynesia." His frown deepened. He never appeared to enjoy the prospect of his destinations.

Polynesia. Her mind seemed to float on a purple sea, wash up in warm breakers onto black sand. She had no idea if there were beaches of black sand in Polynesia. She asked him.

He shook his head, holding one of the quail between two index fingers, biting. "You're thinking of Pago Pago."

She threw her head back and laughed, knowing he did not see the humor. "I'm not thinking of anywhere. I've not *been* anywhere. I don't know anything." He knew it all but didn't seem to take credit for his knowledge. He treated it with the same indifference he treated her food or her social life.

Now he was sitting back in his chair, leaning back and craning his neck, looking for their waitress. He couldn't find her. He sighed. "Of course, I have to finish the St. Petersburg section before I leave." He fiddled with his spoon, wanting coffee and dessert.

The *section* was part of the book he was currently working on. She thought it was amazing.

"The most amazing thing."

"What?"

"To write a book. And you've written five or six."

He shrugged and said, "You should try it, then." He leaned back again, tilting the chair and, seeing the waitress, energetically waving his arm.

"Why do you always tell me that? As if one merely had to snap one's fingers and there it would be?"

"What would be?"

He had already forgotten. Not only what she had said about his writing, but what he himself had said in response.

She felt invisible. As if he were speaking, when he spoke, only to empty air. She felt desolate. And once more she told herself she would not meet him again for one of these lunches, knowing that she would.

He had mistaken her for someone else.

That was how they'd met: he had walked over to her table, studied her face, and told her she was the *image* of Mary-Beth, a friend of his.

This had seemed to be important to him, as if the woman and he had been close, yet she had never heard him speak of Mary-Beth again.

She had been eating lunch quite late, around three — something she never did, she rarely ate lunch at all — but this time she'd had no breakfast and had come from her attorney's office.

The attorney had talked at length about her affairs; they were more complex than she had believed. She found it difficult to think of her affairs, or of any other part of her uneventful life, as needing the watchful eye of a lawyer.

At first, she had not liked these midafternoon lunches; she would have preferred meeting later, for dinner. It would have helped to fill the evening hours that always stretched out before her.

It was after the third lunch that she had realized that they had settled into a ritual. But she never understood why. Had they actually enjoyed one another's company so much during that first meal that they had agreed to meet again the following week? And had the following week's lunch been such a success that lunches three, four, five, and so on had settled into this semblance of a ritual? It was not that they found themselves in sympathy with one another, that was clear. She would have said, had there been more consciousness at work, that they set about deliberately to annoy each other. His complicity in this she judged to be less than hers because she saw him as less conscious of it. She felt she maneuvered him into positions that would permit her rook to check his king. Yet she never did because he managed to knock it off the board with some comment that spoke of the impossibility of retrieval. She would stare at him, openmouthed. She was intrigued by her attendance at these meals, especially given the sad realization that for him she could have been anybody. He wanted only a luncheon companion, someone to break bread with, a witness to his selection of meat and wine, an argument to refute.

She did not realize this at first, of course not. The awareness came slowly over many weeks and months of their lunching together. And when it did become clear that he might not even like her, she felt pained and disappointed, but she very soon outgrew the stings of humiliation and became, simply, an observer, an ear to take in their often incoherent conversations, a third party at their table.

FOUR

The waitress never questioned her presence in the Railway Café. If the waitress wondered why she came so often, she kept it to herself. Probably, she even liked it; it meant another person to share the burden of silence, and that was always good. Their talk never rose above comments about the food and sometimes the weather, but that was all right too. There was a sufficiency in these narrow exchanges — "Your cook makes the best grilled cheese"; "Well, I'll tell him you said that" — that she didn't get from listening to even the most intricately styled talks or lectures or conversations. The brief transactions with the waitress were satisfying, just as the grilled-cheese sandwiches and slices of pie were more filling than one of those four-course lunches.

She wondered about the life of the waitress but never asked. She wondered whether she found her job here awfully dull and if she had children, a husband, a home. Or did the waitress live in rooms somewhere? Thinking of her own house, so spacious and empty, she had at times considered turning it into a rooming house. It appealed to her, this picture of herself as a landlady in one of those shapeless brown cardigans, watching her roomers come and go, no one staying for very long, which permitted a flow of fixed arrivals and departures but also allowed for entire lives lived in secret. She did not mean to penetrate those secrets, just as she did not want to discover things about the waitress. She did not look for clues, like a wedding ring or a snapshot stuck in the corner of the mirror that ran the length of the counter. (There *were* a few snapshots there, but she had no idea to whom they belonged.) She was not eager to discover the waitress had a flourishing life away from the café; she did not want a door to open on a larger world, one in which she would have to include the waitress's family: how they looked and what they did and how they felt.

Or, she thought, it might be simple jealousy of the rich and flowing lives of other people, lives which would flow toward her and around her in the form of strangers leaving work, coming out of their cramped offices, free of their jobs, women in the summer dusk in their bright dresses, whole gardens of them.

She was certain (but did not know why) that the waitress was not one of those and was much more like she herself. Had she had to go to work again, she thought she would prefer a very simple job such as waiting on tables. But only in such a place as the Railway Café.

She had said this to her friend as they lunched

in a rather bohemian brasserie that seemed to work hard at keeping its Hungarian ambience. The waitresses wore bright scarves and long multicolored skirts. What she had said to him was that she would hate to wait on tables dressed in costume; she would prefer a plain uniform, light blue or white. She had talked about this at some length, describing the various waitresses and waiters (who wore long scarves around their middles instead of belts, and suspenders), but she knew he wasn't listening. Probably he would consider all of her comments mere badinage and not worth listening to.

She was surprised when he actually commented on what she had said. "Why in God's name would you want to do something as dull as waiting tables? I can't imagine anything duller."

"Really? But you seem to find certain waiters fascinating, I mean, like the sommelier at that French place —"

He barked out a laugh. "A sommelier is *not* a waiter!"

"No, but you enjoy the waiters in that place, too."

He continued to eat his *gulyás,* saying, "Your trouble is you don't have enough to do. What you should do is go back to work."

"But why? I didn't like my work. And I don't need the money."

"You were unlucky in that inheritance."

She frowned. What could he possibly mean? "You make it sound like some bad Victorian novel. The heroine is undone because the man wants only her money. I would hardly call it an inheritance in that sense. It's not a great deal of money." Her father and then her mother had died, and both had left her a substantial amount. Enough to get by on, was what her mother had always said. "That's all," she said to him now, although it was far more than just enough to get by on.

To this he said nothing. He had stopped listening again and was signaling the waiter.

"Not everyone can have a fascinating job like yours."

When he'd finally brought the waiter bearing down on them, he looked at her blankly and asked, "Fascinating how?"

⨍IVE

Another time they lunched in what he said was a restaurant that served good Basque food. But he settled once again for duck. He couldn't seem to get enough of it. On his plate were smoked duck, duck foie gras, and a duck confit.

"You're about as sociable as a hermit." He was craning his neck, leaning back in his chair, trying to locate their waiter.

He enjoyed criticizing her reclusiveness, saying how she might as well be a hermit and live on a mountaintop. Especially as his own life stood in such sharp contrast to hers. Yet, he did not like his life, she was sure of that. But that apparently was beside the point. His life was (he admitted) but one model of how life should be lived.

"I'm not saying everyone should go jumping about the globe the way I do, God forbid. But we have to be out and about."

"I'm very often out and about. I'm right now out and about with you. You accused me of being out and about too much." She meant to the café.

"You're twisting my words. You're being ironic, as usual. You know what I mean."

No, she didn't. *Out and about* did not mean anything.

Finally, he saw the waiter and motioned him to their table with the remonstrating arm of a state trooper waving over a speeding automobile. "Your life," he said, "is too narrow. No man is an island, remember that."

"But Donne wasn't talking about being sociable, he was talking about charity. Or empathy. We must be more charitable, give something of our lives over to it. He was talking about identifying with others, not about throwing a party."

He grunted. "For whom the bell tolls, you mean? We're all in it together, that's what. We all have to pull together."

"I don't think Donne would mind me going to the Railway Café."

The waiter had come and he ordered crème caramel (which didn't sound very Basque to her). When the waiter went away, he leaned across the table. "You've become a recluse, that's all."

It was the recluse monologue, and she tuned it out as best she could. It was not really his carping on the way she lived her life that bothered her. This niggling and picking amused more than angered her. What bothered her was that she could have been anyone. He did not care if the person seated across from him now were she or another; he could have as easily adjusted his criticism to someone, anyone, else. He did not care if she was a recluse, just as he did not care if she enjoyed her lunch. He had simply shifted into talking gear. He did not really care what he said. Of course, he would have denied this with a vengeance.

As he rattled on about the way she spent her life, she fantasized that the gods had apportioned a certain handful of words to each person. Fifty, say. Fifty words for each occasion. If one ran over the fifty words, one would not be allowed to repeat that occasion. She would not be permitted to lunch with him again. She frowned. But what about the other person? What if he did *not* go over the fifty? Should he not be able to repeat the occasion either? This was a problem.

". . . the point is, we must have social encounters." The blade of his butter knife carved a line in the white tablecloth.

"I'm having one right now. With you."

Seven words. Or should she count "I'm" as two and make it eight? Probably she should.

"Look here: I'm only trying to help you. Trying to be your friend. You mustn't keep cooping yourself up the way you do. Oh, yes, you have a meal with me sometimes, but —"

Her figuring could not move as swiftly as his mouth, so she had to guess: "Twenty-five to thirty," she said.

"What? What?"

"Words. I'm playing a game."

"What game? What are you talking about?"

"If each of us were allowed only fifty words to say and no more, could we keep within the bounds of those fifty?"

He stared at her for a moment and then shook his head, feigning pity. "You really live in a no-man's-land, don't you?"

SIX

Perhaps I do, she thought, counting out change for her grilled-cheese sandwich and coffee. Only it wasn't clear just what this particular no-man's-land was.

Yet it might have been the one true thing he'd spoken during that whole long lunch. She had come to realize that having lunch with him meant giving over one's entire afternoon. That would certainly not bankrupt her afternoons, though, as she had few ways of filling them.

They seldom entered the restaurant before three or even four. He always went through four courses. This particular lunch had begun with mussels cooked in some queer way coming before the salad and described in cursive and discursive French, making it near impossible to assimilate the overdesigned mussels. And dessert was not even the end of things, for there were liqueurs to follow, and coffee and a plate of tiny chocolates. These meals would take all afternoon, running up against the dinnertime of most people, or at least their cocktail hour.

She could never have begun to eat all of those

courses. It was not that she was indifferent to food, for she could have put away two or even three of the Railway Café's grilled-cheese sandwiches. Sitting there now, she thought she might even have one later, when she came back for another cup of coffee.

When she went up to the register, the waitress came over and took the check and her money. As she punched down the cash-register keys, she smiled a genuine smile. She did not appear to be bored by her job at all. This was strange, for all she did after her little bit of serving was to position herself at the end of the counter and smoke and look out at the platform.

It had been simple, when she'd first started coming here, to figure out a tip. But it became increasingly difficult because she had come to think of the waitress as — well, perhaps not a friend but a very good acquaintance. She had decided never to leave less than a dollar, even when the check was no more than two or three dollars, which was what it had been today.

She walked the platform now. Even before she heard it, she felt the vibration of the distant train. This would be the train to that city from which one could board a freighter. In another minute, the station manager announced it over the public address system that boomed out indecipherable destinations. No one depended on the station manager's voice for information. Still, these loud muddied announcements served to give the station itself a sense of direction, a raison d'être.

The station manager appeared then with his dolly full of heavy-looking boxes that would be loaded onto the freight cars along with the mail. The boxes on the dolly shivered as the train drew closer. She could see the engine down the line. The station manager would have read off the stops over the loudspeaker, but of course she hadn't understood.

It was a behemoth, nearly screaming when it stopped, spitting up sparks, wheels shrieking with the lurch of the brakes. Peering out from one of the windows were two children, a boy and a girl, their faces pressed against the glass, which had flattened their noses to the shape of snouts. They were staring at her, making her feel vaguely uncomfortable. She changed her position, walked a few feet along, noticing how tired many of the passengers seemed to be, tired or bored. Yet they conveyed the sense of living in a secret world remote from her world's troubles, un-reachable. Some of them were oblivious — to the stop and the station and to her, of course. She wondered if the ones who looked out thought the same as she did, that she inhabited a world from which they were excluded. No, for they were the ones who had stormed the citadel, taken over the castle, found sanctuary.

SEVEN

While he ate his dessert, he said something about the difficulties of writing, how he had run into trouble with a certain section of his book.

At first she thought he was being ironic. Naïvely, she had asked him how, honestly, he could expect to write about a subject he disliked so much and *not* run into trouble.

"I can't think what you're talking about. You simply don't understand the pitfalls of writing, the uncertainty, all of that."

She smiled as she said, "But you're like the guidebook writer in that novel by Anne Tyler."

He was incensed. "I am *not* a writer of guidebooks."

"Of course not! I only meant —" She gave up.

She understood that he was unaware of his true feelings, unaware that everything he said — or didn't say, since he disliked talking about his trips — was more evidence that he hated to travel. And hated writing about it. He did acknowledge a kind of hatred of writing, but he put that down to the troubles that afflict all writers: the blocks, the terror of the empty white page, words like lead and inert sentences into which it sometimes seemed impossible to breathe any life. He had more or less manufactured a monster to account for his writing problems: some untamable, unchainable beast who was fierce but stupid, slavering but toothless, so that one could not even own it as the "beast of the unconscious." It was simply too damned dumb for that (he had said, laughing). After all, the unconscious had a design; it had its methods, its logic.

So his writing troubles were never attributed to his hatred of travel. They were put at the door of the beast. His succulent ideas ended up as picked bones, strewn about a Cyclops' cave.

"And I am *not* as clever as Odysseus." His pale blue eyes grew more intense, as if someone had plugged in an electrical cord and charged them. It was clear that this was just how he saw himself — as clever as Odysseus. He tricked the beast; he had escaped with a decent day's writing.

"Meaning," she said, "you tricked yourself."

"No."

He was unwilling to concede even this obvious point.

"You don't understand, that's all," he said. "But then, you're not a writer."

She sighed and agreed with him. She wasn't a writer. Then she said perhaps he should have become a food writer rather than a travel writer.

No, he enjoyed travel too much, he'd replied.

She felt again that she could not connect with him, could not make contact. It was a charade.

She studied the plate of little chocolates the waiter had brought with the coffee, picked one up, put it down, and felt even lonelier.

EIGHT

On the other side of the café wall behind the grille and the counter was a small kitchen. The cook would pass plates through a hatch, banging up the wooden door as if he had so many orders he had to hurry, when hers was the only order to fill.

In the beginning, the cook had seemed mysterious. She liked to think of him as a fugitive from the world who had chosen the kitchen as his permanent hideout where he could create, undisturbed, a menuful of omelets.

He would emerge, of course, from time to time to pour himself a cup of coffee from one of the Pyrex coffeepots. He would have a cigarette with his coffee. Now there would be two of them standing at the end of the counter, smoking and looking out of the window at the tracks. They did this, both of them, in such concert and with such intensity that at first she had thought surely there must be something happening on the platform. When she turned in her chair to see, nothing was happening. Nothing ever happened, except for the trains arriving and departing, and even then it was a rare occurrence for anyone to get off or on.

While the cook and the waitress leaned side by side against the counter, their talk was minimal, body movements substituting for some of it, taking the place of words. A shrug, a headshake, a hand drawing in air. She was struck by the intimacy of their shared silence, but at the same time she was sure that their relationship was confined to the café. The café gave it meaning. She wondered how the cook felt about his job, given so few customers. What did he do all day in the kitchen when she herself was the only one in the café? She wondered if he was proud of his omelets. She had told the waitress in the beginning how marvelously prepared the omelets were, and the waitress had said she would be sure to tell the cook. Could he keep going on the force of a single compliment? Would he think it was worth the trouble to go on separating the yolks from the whites? Only her mother had made omelets in this way, beating the whites to stiff meringue. Now her mother was dead.

She thought of her mother more, not less, over the years and felt increasingly bereft. The years faded behind her, details slipping away. She felt she too was fading into the background, her outline becoming less clear, like a figure in a tapestry, uncertain and underwrought. It was as much as a person could do to keep the dim colors of self from fading altogether.

She had the chilly feeling that beyond these

walls, lives could unravel if one weren't exceedingly watchful, careful about retracing the pattern, like children mindful of stepping into the outlines of their own footprints. Like those two, she thought, looking at the waitress and cook: once they left at the end of the day, they would go home to sleep until the next day, when they would wake and come back again. It was the only safe way.

It had been snowing that day, snow mixing with rain, an iridescent pattern. The restaurant was Ukrainian and was down in a cellar which darkened an already darkening afternoon. But she liked it, the interior; it suited her mood.

She had chosen it because he had recently returned from Odessa and she thought it fitting. With a bit of contempt, he called it one of her finds, adding, "where we can rub elbows with the help." The staff of her chosen restaurants were always *the help*. But he seemed satisfied when he saw the menu and could proclaim it a pretty authentic-looking selection of dishes. She knew the food would be heavy, even the brothlike soup weighed down by noodles. But she did not mind, for the restaurant fit her mood, if not her appetite.

As were the other places where they ate, this one was nearly empty at this hour. She pointed out that the only elbow rubbing they could do was with the group of men sitting across the room, far enough away that their words could be heard only in snatches — when one of them laughed and raised his voice. Otherwise, their talk was a mere murmur, which she found pleasant, a sound that reminded her of the discourse beneath a running stream.

After he set aside the menu and was picking up the wine list, he made a comment about the weather here where they were and how different it was in the Ukraine. What he said was that in Odessa the temperature had fallen to the point where the crosses were so encased in ice they looked like mirror spindles and he thought his hands would crack, as if he were wearing glass gloves.

She was astonished, for he scarcely ever spoke in metaphor; she told him he had just conjured up a perfect picture and wanted him to go on, but he wouldn't. Instead, he gave a short bark of laughter and asked what was there, after all, to say about a place like Odessa or Constanta?

"But if you just *said — ?*" she persisted.

He didn't comment; he gave her one of his annoying little shrugs and examined the wine list.

She knew it was hopeless trying to get more out of him. So her interest was drawn back to the far table where the three men sat — businessmen, she judged, from the way they were dressed. All three were smoking cigars and had globes of brandy in front of them. She was irrationally glad the restaurant permitted cigar-smoking, for they seemed to be enjoying them so much. When she turned back to their own table, he was still poring over the wine list, and she wondered if this gave him the sort of comfort smoking a cigar would. She resumed her study of the businessmen who seemed so thoroughly to be enjoying themselves. She would have liked to sit with them; she envied them their easy friendship and relaxed posture. She would have liked to be not the entertainer so much as the entertained.

And then she thought of an old photograph she had of her father, long dead, and whom she had known hardly at all. Whom she could barely remember. The photograph was of him and three other men — young men — all gathered on a riverbank. Yet there seemed no reason at all for that setting, for they weren't dressed for swimming or fishing, as all of them were dressed in business suits. All smiled broadly, all with their trousers rolled above their ankles and their feet in the water. She kept this snapshot stuck into a mirror frame, often wondering what had brought these four young men to this river, dressed this way. Had they been on their way to work or to some social gathering? Had they, on a lark, decided to stop and go to the bank of the river? Wherever they had come from or were going, they all had the same childlike look of freedom from constraint — much like the businessmen at the far table. If her father had lived, would there have been the jokes and easy talk she heard at that table? She thought, yes, there would have been. But she had no reason to think so, except for the snapshot and the way he was smiling.

The waiter had come to take their orders, and she carelessly asked for a meat salad. He, of course, ordered far more extensively, choosing for his main course a heavily marinated meat, which he told her was like sauerbraten, which he really would have preferred; he could go for a nice plate of sauerbraten and could have had it, too, if they'd gone to his German restaurant. He sighed heavily, dramatically. He had ordered a red wine, another one of those "village appellations" because there wasn't much to choose from here. He sighed again, turning crosswise in his chair to look at empty air.

He was not placed, as she was, so that he could easily see the businessmen. She could watch them without being seen to watch. It was unlikely that they would care, anyway. The weight of their talk had shifted from the one in the middle to the one on his right, who then appeared to entertain the others with equal ease.

They were perfect strangers to her, and yet it made her anxious to see the first fluttering signs of their departure: napkins being tossed onto the table, the last of the brandy drunk, the searching looks for the waiter, the checking of watches and laughing. She looked away down at her glass of simple village wine. Her throat felt tight and she raised it to take a sip.

Then she returned to the subject of the Ukraine cold, knowing he had said all he cared to. "I've never been to Odessa, and I've never even heard of Constanta."

He nodded, as if this were a reasonable observation. "You might like that part of the world. You should go." He drank his wine.

In dismay she shut her eyes tightly. For he knew perfectly well she wouldn't go. She said so.

"Why not? You have the money for it."

She started to say, You know that's not the point, but caught herself. For that would permit him to involve her in an argument. Any further talk about Russian winters would be lost. He loved to sidetrack her, to derail her so that she'd never get where she was headed. She tried to imagine Odessa and its icy crosses. "Is it on the Black Sea?"

"Is what?" He was examining a hunk of black bread the waiter had dropped on the table.

"O-des-sa." She translated her irritation into three distinct syllables.

He ignored the emphasis on the name and buttered his bread.

In her mind's eye she pictured the crosses in the sun as sharply bright as glass. And snow, the level unbroken crust of it, the black trees, a park unpeopled. But she gave it up; she hadn't the imagination.

Across the room, the businessmen had risen and were searching their pockets and wallets for money, which they tossed on the table for the tip and then walked toward the door. All of this was accomplished without a break in their talk or a missed beat in their laughter.

She watched them openly now, and at the door one of them glanced back at her and smiled as if to say, *Take heart.*

NINE

Several months ago, when he had returned from his Polynesian jaunt (which is what he called them, *jaunts,* as if to deny them any status and thus to demean them), they had lunched again, this time in a restaurant with an arctic feel to it, full of glass and chrome, granite, and white marble. Yet the menu was surprisingly familiar. Did every restaurant in the world do something odd with mussels? she had asked him.

"Why? Don't you like them?" His tone was suspicious, as if every question she put to him could be a trap, might have a bomb hidden in it.

"That's not the —" *Point* was what she'd been going to say. But he would take that as an attack upon his reasoning and get defensive, and they would end up arguing over mussels. Rather, *he* would end up arguing. It was easier to answer simply, but even there the answer had better be yes, for if she said no, they would end up arguing anyway. "Yes," she answered.

"Then why," he slyly asked, "didn't you order them? Since you like them?"

He always won.

"I wanted the asparagus today. It's awfully good." She pointed her fork at the thin spears, their middle bathed in hollandaise. "Tell me about your trip." He wouldn't, of course, but the question served to distract him from the mussel argument.

He shrugged. "Same old stuff." He broke off a piece of a baguette and dipped it in the winy mussel liquor. "Unseasonably hot. And a *lot* of rain. So much you wake up and all your clothes are moldy." He emphasized this, as if it were the most interesting detail he could toss out. He had got a sliver of something caught in a tooth and set about applying his gold toothpick to it.

"I didn't know Tahiti had seasons."

"Of course it does. Everywhere has seasons. You just have to know how to look for them."

Delightful images formed in her mind and she smiled. She saw the seasons hiding: spring behind a tree, winter in the attic, summer in the shrubbery. "I suppose I always thought of places like that as *temperate*. In the temperate zone." She smiled at him, but he didn't notice. He was still working on his tooth, politely covering this little operation behind his other hand. Then he added, "Winter is dry." He plied the toothpick.

The asparagus was quite good, but she rarely had an appetizer at lunch. To take care of the next two courses, she had ordered a seafood salad that would serve as both. It was a sensible selection, but he still found something to criticize in it. She should eat something hot. He complained about this cold dish for a moment or two; then, finding it a dull subject for an argument, let it go, even though dullness ordinarily didn't stop him.

As their salads were set before them, she returned to the seasons of the islands. "Perhaps it's more like a monsoon season." Had he heard her? He was fixing his attention on his fruit salad: papaya and orange segments and arugula and poppy-seed dressing. She said, "But it must be beautiful — I mean, those islands — whatever the season."

He had heard her this time and might seriously have been considering her comment, for he threw back his head and looked at the ceiling. This was evidence of concentration. But she considered her comment about beauty, when applied to a place such as Tahiti, to be utterly banal and surely unarguable. Yet he seemed to be about to argue, given the energetic attention he was now paying the room. After a few more moments of wall-and-ceiling study, he shook his head and said, "Not as beautiful as Maui."

This surprised her. "But I thought Maui didn't impress you at all!"

"I don't think I said that, precisely. Oh, it *impressed* me, all right. But not overly much." He tapped his mouth with his napkin several times, looking beyond her to the shadeless glare of the window. "The point is, you see, not some Platonic notion of what you call *beauty* but an ineffable, indefinable, and, I would say, fleeting

61

quality. Those ubiquitous blues and greens, which you're associating with Tahiti, are indeed relatively faded but nonetheless pure. It's that purity that attracts and transcends its own attraction. 'Beauty is momentary in the mind, the fitful' " — he paused, searching the air for the word — " 'the fitful'. . . something of a something, as Wallace Stevens would say. You know the poem." He speared an orange segment.

She blinked, utterly astonished by the length of this answer, to say nothing of its substance — the lines of Wallace Stevens that he had brandished about with as little concern as he had for the orange segment. Yet he seemed quite satisfied with his meaning and went on eating his salad, now and then pausing to rid it of a dried cranberry. For a moment or two she attempted to tidy up his little speech, as he did his salad, but could gain no mental foothold. Either she was extremely dense or he had said absolutely nothing.

His airy language appeared to sustain him as much as his fruit salad did. She would rather have thought he was laughing at her by means of his verbose and meaningless definition; this would at least have implied a deeper thinking on his part than she had ever found him capable of. She would prefer to think he was being ironic, calling her bluff, perhaps, for persisting in her bourgeois notion of beauty. And calling on Wallace Stevens on top of it! It was the only time he had ever quoted poetry. He wasn't an ironist;

he was a literalist to the core. He would leave her to flounder and flail. He himself had no depths; he could not go down. He lived, in a manner of speaking, horizontally, like a man floating on a boundless sea whose ballooning garments kept him from sinking.

She pressed her temples. She was getting as bad as he; it was as if her interior voices had decided to speak in tongues. "Oh, my! —" She gave a weak laugh.

"What's wrong?"

"Nothing more than a mild headache."

"I take it you disagree."

"Disagree?" She was immediately wary.

"With what I said about the idea of beauty." He glanced at her crossly.

Oh, dear. She could not say, simply, no. He would worry it like a little dog. She could add something to it. "I was thinking of that Stevens poem. It's quite interesting."

"Opaque," he announced.

Now she was altogether puzzled. Why, then, had he quoted from it?

"Opaque," he said again. "I sometimes wonder if Stevens" — he paused to rid his salad of another cranberry bit — "was really talking about anything at all."

TEN

In the library she had found a small book of Wallace Stevens's poetry and now took it out of her bag in the Railway Café. She was lingering over her midafternoon cup of coffee and had decided to have a grilled-cheese sandwich with it.

Beauty is momentary in the mind —
The fitful tracing of a portal;
But in the flesh it is immortal.

This was wonderful, she thought, but difficult. She was surprised, more than anything, by his having referred to it. She would have thought Wallace Stevens would be irrelevant to him. And there were the words he hadn't remembered. It had not occurred to him, apparently, that one could hardly leave out even one word and still have the poem mean the same thing.

She sighed and closed the book and returned it to her bag. She picked up the last quarter of her sandwich and thought about that lunch. What she thought was: You continue lunching with him because you feel superior. That made her feel rather hopeless, for if she felt superior, there was no possibility of communication, because one would already have given up. This worried her, and she looked around for the waitress.

The waitress and the cook were standing side by side at the end of the counter looking out at the freight train that was sparking and clanging, as if it were in full motion even though it had stopped. The stationmaster was standing by the track with a luggage carrier on which sacks of mail had sat before they were conveyed to one of the cars. Inside the freight car, one man, his T-shirt sleeves rolled to his shoulder, was lifting up and handing down one of the cartons into the arms of another worker on the platform. He in turn set the carton on the carrier.

She admired this act; it was simple, and the role of each was clearly assigned. She watched (together with the cook and the waitress) while they heaved each carton up and down and over, treating them with great care, as if the contents were fragile. When they were done, the train gathered up power and moved creakily on the track, as if now it was reluctant to go and would sit here and test its own strength.

Then the café door was thrown open, admitting a group of young people, high schoolers or perhaps college students; it was hard to tell their ages. For a period of her life she had taught in the local high school until she could no longer stand it. She had seen a few of them before in the café. Either these or others would burst in sometimes at the weekend, noisily, like inmates out of prison working off their energy. They were boisterous and proprietorial, immediately dragging chairs around, shoving tables together. She could not imagine what attracted them to this café. It served no alcohol, not even beer, and these young people were clearly fueled by it. Did they like it precisely because it was so quiet and uninteresting that they felt they could more easily master it? They were clamorous, unassailable, and could not be still even when sitting. What they said or yelled to one another might have been spoken in a foreign tongue. As if by fiat, their actions declared they could do anything they wanted. They tossed things about, pitched packs of cigarettes and matches through the air; they hauled over still more chairs to clamp their feet upon. The girl at the end of the table, the loudest of all, was probably their unofficial leader. All packs had one. She was dressed completely in black: boots, jeans, satin shirt, and a wide-brimmed hat. It was she who called out to the waitress.

She would never have been able to stand up to this crew, undoubtedly high schoolers. They looked older, but over the years all children seemed to her to look increasingly older. If she had had this crowd to deal with in a classroom, she knew she would have simply run from the school. The inheritance left her by her parents she now thanked God for. It made her ashamed, this admission, even to herself, and she turned her hot face to the Stevens book.

The waitress moved to their table with her characteristic languor and took out her pad, completely unruffled by their appearance or by their demands or their comments. Clearly, they were baiting her by making disparaging comments about the café. The group seemed to see itself in the light of ancient Greek troops, sackers of cities. But the waitress neither scowled nor smiled. Her self-possession was exquisite. Finally, expressionless, she tucked her pencil behind her ear and walked away, but paused fractionally as she looked across the room and winked.

It was as if they shared a secret, their assessment of the raucous teenagers, but more than that: a secret of survival.

ELEVEN

"La Paz? The Amazon? I wasn't even sure the Amazon was in Bolivia!" She said this, looking up from her menu.

The restaurant was a small and simple one, Italian. The round tables were covered with red-and-white checked cloths, and on each was a water glass full of thin dry breadsticks. The green plants were plastic and a little dusty. Only rarely did they lunch at a restaurant she herself had chosen, and this was one of them. She realized that whatever comfort she could draw from eating in a restaurant that was small, warm, and familiar would be extinguished during the course of the meal by his criticizing the place.

Now he heaved a sigh and said, "I can't think why you like it here. Here's pasta with fifteen different sauces and that's about all."

Her own sigh was one of comfort rather than of distress. "Remember when we called it all spaghetti?"

Frowning over the top of his menu, he said, "It's pasta. Spaghetti's only one kind."

He was so literal. "I know, but there was a time when we — surely I'm not the only one! — carelessly called all of it plain spaghetti, and that included the sauce too. Meat sauce or meatballs. I'm going to ask for that, tomato sauce and meatballs."

With a snort and a smile that was more of a sneer, he said, "Going to be disappointed, then. It's not on here." He waved the menu at her. Scoring a tiny victory. Recompense for having to eat in this undistinguished place.

Spaghetti and meatballs. That provoked in her a dreaminess, and she closed her eyes. When she opened them he was still scouring the menu.

The waiter came, and she asked him if it was possible to get spaghetti and meatballs, instead of meat sauce. Politely he told her, in heavily accented English, that he thought the chef could see to it.

Her friend slapped down the menu and said, "I'll start with the antipasto — there's no calamari in it, is there? I hate it." The waiter assured him there was none. "Then I'll have linguine with mussels." The waiter smiled and left.

Was that *really* on the menu? She peeked inside hers again to see. Yes, it was. But she made no comment.

He was busy munching a breadstick, which he declared not only stingy but tasteless; he was craning his neck to stare around the room. He finally settled on listening to the conversation at the table near theirs. But the man and woman were speaking in tones too low for him, lean back as he would, pressing his ear against air.

"When are you leaving?"

His eyebrows shot up as if he didn't understand the question, then he did, and said, "Next week."

"Bolivia. The Amazon. It sounds wonderful."

"Yes, well, you can say so. You don't have to go there."

Surprised, she sat back. "Have to? But they don't order you to visit a certain place, do they?" *They* were an uncertain entity; *they* might comprise editors or publishers or public relations people or all of these. "After all, you're not writing magazine pieces!"

"Thank God!" His laugh was raspy.

"You're writing whole *books*." It astonished her that he had published six of these — or was it seven? And that they were considered to be quite solid and informative and had a healthy readership. She herself had a hard time getting into them, but she considered that to be her fault, not his. She was dismayed by travel writing. She fantasized about exotic places, yes, as did everyone. But the notion of actually packing one's bags and setting off for these places was beyond her capability. Her senses would be bombarded; she would be confused by directional signs; she would be looking only for a place to sit down. "They can't order you to this place or that."

"No, not precisely." He was holding a breadstick in each hand, inspecting first one, then the other. "There were places they suggested. Egypt was one; Austria was one. You know, the Nile, the Danube. They want a piece about a river this time. Too much screwing around on land, so they want a river."

"But —" She was baffled that *they* appeared to be as vague in their wishes as he was in fulfilling them. And yet the books got written, the books got edited, the books got published. And sold. She could not say why, but she felt she must raise some objection to this hit-or-miss way of writing and publishing. Yet she certainly did not wish to get into any discussion of the writing process. So she would stick simply with him and his next destination. Wasn't there a rain forest in Bolivia? And did the Amazon River flow through it? Pictures floated into her mind, floated because she imagined herself in a long bark canoe, moving along the river, between banks lush with green fronds and thick hanging vines, birds with feathers of blinding brightness, and she would see all of this in the blue shadows. . . . Then she imagined a call that rent the air, a splash of water, a scream. She shivered. She watched him using the hard, thin bread like drumsticks, *rat-ta-tat-tat,* beating on the table's edge.

Although she had no reason to think he was a coward, neither did she think he was a courageous man. Thus, this possibly unaccompanied trip on the Amazon River struck her as totally at odds with his nature. He did not like taking chances. Even her choice of restaurant made him nervous. He was always edgy on the short trip from entrance to table, following a maître d' or, as in this day's unpretentious restaurant, one of the waiters. He would whisper things like, "They all look alike, don't they? They're a family, it's family run, so you know the type of food we'll get." Right behind her he walked, almost stepping on her heels, as if they'd got lost on safari and found themselves at the mercy of an untrustworthy guide. He seemed, on these excursions into *her* restaurants or cafés, absolutely to depend on her to get them out alive.

"Do you go alone, then, on this trip?" she asked, while he went on *rat-a-tat*-ing with the breadsticks, and *ping*-ing on the edge of his water glass. The cymbal, apparently. She put her hand on his, annoyed. "I wish you'd pay attention."

"What? Where in hell's our food? How long does it take to get stuff out of jars and slide it on a plate? Bet you. Nothing's homemade. That's where these family-run places fool you. So? Pay attention to what? Were you talking? No."

She was getting a headache. "I asked you a question. Are there others going on this jaunt with you? Surely, you'll have a guide?"

But he seemed uninterested. He had pulled over the wine list in its deep red cover. "We forgot the wine. What were you saying?"

"A *guide*. Will you have a guide?"

"Probably."

"Because you can hardly make such a trip as

that alone. Not even Marlowe did that!"

"Who?"

"Marlowe. *Heart of Darkness.*"

"Ah, yes. Kurtz and so forth. What do you say to a bottle of Pouilly-Fuissé?"

She thought he was being just a little cavalier about Kurtz, with his *and so forth.* In her own mind she could see dark shapes come alive in the dimness and move toward his fragile boat so noiselessly that they barely parted the water, then the gleam of ivory teeth. Wasn't that what Conrad meant? The savage light of civilization? They pressed toward her, quietly, inexorably. She tried to rid her skin of the chill by wiping her hands up and down her upper arms. "The thing is, it's dangerous."

But he was calling the waiter over to take his wine order. The Pouilly-Fuissé after all. He did not really need her acquiescence.

She repeated her comment. "I *said,* isn't it dangerous?"

He shrugged, dismissively. "Parts of it may be. I should have ordered the Burgundy. Damn." He had the wine list open again.

"Yes, but *which* parts? And which parts will you be traveling?"

His eyes now were on the waiter approaching with their wine. "I hope this bottle has enough body to stand up to the pasta." After the waiter poured, he went through his ritual of gazing, twirling, and tasting. It took him a long time to determine its acceptability. Finally, he nodded and gestured for the waiter to pour.

It was a subject — wine — about which he could speak not only authoritatively but concretely. He always studied the wine list with a good deal of concentration before he chose. The wine was perfectly good, although, knowing so little about it and having drunk so few outstanding wines, she was not at all sure she could trust her palate. Several times she had pronounced a wine especially good that he had denounced as being too vinegary, or from a chancy year, or from a suspect vineyard.

All of this he claimed he had learned during his time in Burgundy. He had known little about the subject before he'd gone there. And he had suggested that she go there too. She should keep her eye on a certain slope near Puligny-Montrachet.

She could not help looking at him in disbelief. A certain slope? Not only would she never see that certain slope, she would not see Burgundy; she would not even see France. When she said this, he pretended astonishment, a great lifting of his eyebrows. Why not? She was solvent, wasn't she? She had her inheritance, hadn't she? But she could not leave places so readily as he, kick the earth off her shoes, as it were. To this he had made his usual gesture of dismissal and said he doubted that was so at all. His was the attitude adults take with children, assuring them the bogey-man was not under the bed, but finding themselves unable to prove it, since bogey-men were capable of vanishing in an instant. Well, she might be a child, but he was certainly not an adult. It astonished her, his assumption that anyone could do what he was doing. It showed a lack of vanity, true, but also a callous disregard for others' limitations. Probably, he would make the point again, if he lingered over his first taste of wine. She hoped not.

Impossible now to pursue the Amazon trip. She changed the subject. "So you must have finished your chapter on Tahiti?"

"Tahiti." He nodded, apparently finding the breadsticks irresistible. He was drumming again, but quietly.

"Well, did you scratch up a . . . theme for it?" She did not know how else to put it. The antipasto had arrived, anyway, and saved him from answering. She waited a few moments while he collected eggplant and salami on his plate. She herself took a black olive. She didn't care for antipasto. Then she asked, "What is it?"

"What's what?" He was fussily tucking a napkin under his chin.

"Whatever the *theme* is you found."

"Oh, that. Beauty. Surprising, but you were a bit of help there."

She stared at him. *Beauty?* This astounded her even more than his saying she'd been a help. Beauty? Surely not. Surely not inspired by that incomprehensible little speech he'd made in which he mauled the Wallace Stevens poem? Apparently, yes. For he was doing it again.

Wielding another breadstick, he recited: "Beauty is momentary in the mind — The fitful something, something, something." He stroked the breadstick down on each "something." "That's what started me off. You brought up Maui. You said I wasn't impressed by it."

That he remembered the conversation surprised her as much as his acting on it, finding something "writable" in it.

He went on: "It got me thinking about beauty being relative."

"Tahiti and Maui, you mean? I don't see how —"

"No, no, not exactly."

The waiter interrupted with two plates of steaming pasta and then sailed off again. She said nothing until he'd had time to get oriented around his linguine.

She asked him. "What did you say about beauty?"

Dexterously, he was rolling linguine around his fork into a perfect knob with no loose ends. "What did I say? Pretty much what I told you before."

She sighed. "Oh. That." Hopeless.

TWELVE

Sometimes she tried to imagine the world of "they."

She was sitting on one of the platform's benches, looking across the tracks to the bench on the other side where a middle-aged couple sat, not speaking.

The world of "they." "They" occupied elaborate offices in a glass and concrete building. High up, with views of parks and rivers. They appeared in her mind as youngish, energetic men forever snatching up parts of manuscripts and putting them down. They rarely sat at their desks; they were usually on the move, always in a hurry.

She did not know how it worked, his relationship with "they." She had tried to get him to particularize "them." He must (she had said) have a specific editor he reported to. Was his editor male or female? (She couldn't picture him dealing with a woman.) He managed to evade the question. He rarely talked about the mechanics of publishing, except in his usual vague terms. *They say they might want to bring this one out in the spring.*

She found it interesting that there were publishing seasons. Spring, summer, fall, winter. She would sit on one of the benches that lined the platform and make whimsical guesses at what each "season" produced. Would autumn be ushered in with leaves of books drifting down to carpet the ground? Would winter produce snowballed books lying forgotten in high drifts, or bestsellers that readers could throw at each other and watch them splatter and disintegrate? Would spring come in with tiny new books sprouting from bookshelves like rows of beans?

So she would sometimes entertain herself there on the railway platform, thinking about the mysterious "they" with their indefinite plans and strange agendas.

She liked the platform. It was uncluttered empty space, stretching, like the tracks, as far as the eye could see. Nothing on it except a few benches and the cart sometimes stacked with mail and cartons, but often empty even of these. Once in a while a passenger got on and another passenger got off. It was as if there must be an even distribution of weight if balance were to be maintained.

How odd that a railway station, usually the picture of rush and bustle and anxious waiting, would be a better place for thinking than one's own room or the library. In the library, people seemed to want to make their presence felt and so were continuously coughing, scraping their chairs, walking about, clearing their throats, whispering. As if, lacking the opportunity for normal discourse, they had to check on themselves to see if they still existed.

On the platform, they withdrew. Too late now to change things; the plan is made, the ticket bought, the bags packed, the die cast, no looking back. Like the middle-aged couple on this particular day, sitting on the other side of the tracks. Still as statues, they neither spoke nor looked at each other. Once in a while they turned their heads to see down the track, he to the right and she to the left, as if even the direction of the train's approach were in question.

Then the air was shattered, abraded by the loudspeaker. The microphone rent the air, crackled as if it were being torn, and then gave way to the voice of the stationmaster and his announcement, "Train arriving on Track Two from —" Here, the words broke, faded, were indecipherable. Always at this important juncture, one understood nothing. It fascinated her, the way the voice became less distinct and fulsome and grew more nasal until it faded away completely.

Down the track the train charged. The man and woman across the tracks looked at each other and spoke to each other for the first time. Of course, she couldn't hear them, but she knew they were asking whether this was their train. He shrugged, she rose halfway, he pulled her down. *Did he say if it's ours? Did you understand that? Where — ? I don't know, couldn't make it out.*

Why can't these people speak clearly?

The train stopped, stayed, but impatiently. The couple boarded. The train made enormous noises, clattered and moaned, spit out sparks, and began to gather its power for a further assault on the tracks. The loudspeaker crackled again: "Train now departing on Track Two for —" The voice faded and the words broke into pieces. It entertained her to imagine that the station-master, having forgotten the towns and cities this train had gone through, was now making up other names, hoping no one would realize. The train arriving, though, did not present so much of a problem as the one departing. At least on the arriving train, one was there and meant to stay. Presumably, the conductor spoke more clearly than the stationmaster. But for the departing train, it was a different story, for they had only the stationmaster to depend on. She had seen departing passengers look at each other in puzzlement. *Is this ours? Is this train going to — ? Perhaps we should go in. . . .*

It amused her to fabricate destinations. *The train now departing for Tahiti . . . Maui . . . Aix-en-Provence . . . La Paz. . . .* And she would imagine her friend dashing up to the ticket window to ask the stationmaster to repeat all of the destinations.

THIRTEEN

Their empty pasta plates were removed by a busboy. They had been handed dessert menus, and coffee had replaced the plates.

She had been thinking again that she had to admire him for never telling her, in answer to her questions, "Read the book." Of course, her questions about his trip were often asked before he'd written the book. As often, though, she questioned him about past trips. Most writers, even the modest ones, must surely be egocentric enough to say, "It's right there in the book. Didn't you read the book?"

Perhaps — it was a strange explanation — he didn't *want* to remember the books any more than he wanted to remember the places. Yet, in writing about his destinations, he appropriated them; in some small way, he made them his own. But she shouldn't have voiced this opinion, for he saw it as still another thing to argue about.

"That's just ridiculous," he had said, when the waiter padded off. He was looking at the menu. "Trouble with you is, you're one of those people who thinks trips are parables. Metaphors of discovery. Well, they aren't." He put down the menu.

She flushed. "I don't think that." Did she?

"At the very least, you think trips should be instructive." He would force her to admit to some kind of wrong thinking.

"But wouldn't anyone think that? That trips should be instructive?"

He sighed and picked up the menu again. "Forgive me for not being Kurtz for you."

Was that an answer? She was baffled. But this was always his way in discourse. He steered to his own line, apparently uncomprehending of what anyone else meant, and he could steer into any fresh stream or inlet he chose.

"No, I don't see you coming back with a necklace of shrunken heads." She gazed down at her espresso, black and thick, and dropped the shaving of lemon into it.

In his throat he made a dismissive sound.

She went on. "Or Marlowe, either. I don't expect you to be Marlowe." She stirred sugar into the coffee and wondered if that was exactly true.

"The problem is, you've some stereotype in your mind —"

"Of what? I've never even remotely come in contact with places like that little village in Burgundy —"

"Tahiti. Polynesia. The Tuamotus. Don't tell me you have no pictures in your head about *that* part of the world!"

It was as if she'd been trying to deceive him

about her lack of knowledge. "I've never even *heard* of the Tuamotus."

But he kept on talking. "The trouble is, you want these places to be more than they are."

Her question rang out: "More than they are *what?* That's my point. *What* are they? You don't —" She stopped, realizing how foolish it would be to say, *You don't describe them.* The man wrote *books* about these places, after all. So what did she mean? Fingers laced tight around her little cup, she stared at the candle inside its red globe.

"I 'don't' what? What were you about to say?"

"Nothing. Nothing." Why had she started this? It was ridiculous. She had read bits and pieces of his books, dipped into them, not out of loyalty but out of curiosity. She had been surprised that the voice in these books was so utterly different from the voice across the table. The writing voice was enthusiastic, curious, at times almost sunny, totally preoccupied with the details of his journey. Waterlogged, almost. Heavy with detail. The temperature of the seawater at the edge of a black sand beach; the pattern of a shawl worn by an old native woman in Mauritius. Her hat, its color, blood orange.

He himself saw no discrepancy between his writing self and his dining self, his social self.

She finished her statement. "You don't think these destinations are more than what you write them up to be?" That sounded too much like criticism. An invitation to an argument.

Yet he missed it. "My Lord, no! If anything, they're less. I'm having dessert. You?"

She breathed more easily. Back on safe ground. "What are you having?" She didn't really feel like dessert, but she'd order nonetheless. Food was very often a fine defense against quarreling.

"I can tell you what I'm *not* having! Tiramisu. A year ago it was chocolate mousse on every menu. Now it's tiramisu."

Feeling quite puffed up that she was able to recite chapter and verse from one of his books, she said, "Aha! But you loved it in that little village in the north of Italy."

His eyes did not leave the menu as he asked, "What little village?"

FOURTEEN

One day the waitress spoke to her. She spoke with a little sigh, as if the conversation which had been interrupted could now continue. When the waitress noticed the book of poetry, she spoke of an old high school teacher, one who had given very dramatic readings of a poet whose name she couldn't recollect.

Beauty is momentary in the mind: that's what she had been thinking when the waitress came as usual to take her order. The waitress liked poetry too but had never read anything by Wallace Stevens.

" 'Beauty is momentary in the mind.' " The waitress's brow furrowed. Both of them looked at the line in the book. The waitress rubbed the hair around her ear with her pencil, still frowning. No, it was too deep.

Once again, she ordered the omelet. The waitress simply nodded and wrote on her pad as if it hadn't been requested two or three times a week.

"I think perhaps I'll take the *herb* omelet today."

The waitress nodded and wrote again on her pad. It was clear she wrote *herb* because of the way she pursed up her mouth, silently saying it. Then she gathered up the menu and trod off on quiet rubber-soled feet.

> *Beauty is momentary in the mind —*
> *The fitful tracing of a portal;*
> *But in the flesh it is immortal.*

She frowned slightly, rested her chin on her fist, and looked out the steamed-up window by her table. What does it mean, a "portal"? A lighted window, literally, but what else?

She always sat at the same table. When there were others in the *café* — today two more tables were occupied — they were never shown to this table, "her" table. Rain glazed the window. It was quite chilly on the platform, but the warmth in the café had steamed the window over, halfway up, where she could see the word café in a half-moon of white letters. This setting reminded her again of *Brief Encounter*. It would never happen to her, such an encounter, she knew. *Don't go about expecting too much, not if you're wise.* The abrasive inner voice was probably her mother's, sad-eyed and certain. Her mother had been downcast about life, had viewed it as a long downward slide. Still, her mother had only wanted to save her daughter from disappointment, not understanding that disappointed hopes would be a certainty if one expected such disappointments. It was not her mother's fault if her own life had been so utterly without incident.

Her uneventful life made her close her eyes tightly and flush, momentarily filled with a sense of shame. It was as if she had wronged herself in some way and was being punished for it. Her fingers pleated the tablecloth, and she was cheered by its starched whiteness. It was so unexpected to see tablecloths in such a café. Of course, the cloth was covered over by a clear vinyl that went at an angle to the white cloth. They couldn't always be changing these tablecloths. They were spotlessly clean. It must be that the waitress and the cook took a lot of pride in the place, even though they were not the owners. At least she didn't think they were. The things that sat in the middle of each table were wiped clean too: salt and pepper shakers, sugar bowl, catsup bottle. The sugar bowl was one of the old-fashioned kind with a hinged chrome lid. She especially liked that. And the whole scene was heightened by the waitress's crisp, clean uniform and the cook's apron. How did they do this? she wondered. More to the point, why did they do it? Why did they care so much?

She inspected, in a series of artful glances, the couples at the other two tables, to see if they would be candidates for *Brief Encounter*. Not the couple in the corner who were reading newspapers, bored with whatever news they might convey to each other.

The man and woman in the film had been so

pleasantly ordinary, so overwhelmed by what was happening to them. That couldn't happen today, could it? Men and women feeling such guilt and grief over the hurt they were inflicting on their own mates? It was hard to imagine a woman today fleeing blindly from a house because the lover's friend had returned without warning. Hard to imagine anyone today would care. The couple near the door in their too-heavy clothes, tweed suit and gray wool? An anachronism, surely. Yes, that couple might fit the roles.

She felt a sharp prick of loss and then the waitress was there, setting the omelet in front of her.

Beauty is momentary in the mind.

FIFTEEN

She asked him again about the *tzanta,* the shrunken head.

Without raising his eyes from the menu — Indian, this time — he said, "Most people don't have a clue about shrunken heads. I think I'll try the shrimp in coconut sauce."

She stared at him. "*I* certainly haven't. A clue, I mean."

Slapping open the wine list, he said, "The ones you're used to seeing? The ones in the stalls in the bazaars? Fakes, all of them."

"The ones I'm 'used to seeing'?"

"Monkey heads. Either that or they're made out of some old bit of canvas. So don't let yourself be taken in." He was running his finger down the list and making either pleasurable sounds or giving grunts of displeasure.

"It's highly unlikely."

"Hmm? What is?"

"How could I be taken in?" She slid the fussily tasseled menu out of her way. "By a fake shrunken head?" Whatever on earth made him say things like that? As if the minute she'd left home, she might have run into a stall where shrunken heads were bartered?

He gave her a level look. "No, I guess not."

The implication in his tone was that she wasn't sufficiently interesting to be bargaining for shrunken heads. And once again she was baffled by his assumption that she must surely at one time have been where he'd been, seen what he'd seen. She asked him, "How do you tell, then?"

"Hmm?" Now he was twisted around in his seat, looking over his shoulder, trying to engage the waiter's eyes.

"How do you tell the difference? Between the real and the fake shrunken head?" What an absurd topic it sounded now. And she didn't really want to know the infernal process; this was only to keep him talking.

He was again bringing the weight of his knowledge to bear on the wine list. "Takes a week to do one. Well, five days at least."

The waiter appeared, diffident, with his poor English. The poor fellow had to recite the long list of specials, and his syllables were lost in the jungle of so many choices. She made out a fish dish somewhere in his spoken list, a curry, but was afraid it might be vindaloo and too hot. Not understanding most of what the waiter said, she ordered from the menu: the vegetarian platter. She did not want him to think she hadn't understood, for he might also have a small speech problem.

Yet, he made the waiter repeat the entire list, his hand cocking his ear and frowning, as if the poor accent and stumbling syllables made choice impossible. He must hear each dish distinctly. It took a good five minutes (she was curious, and looked at her watch) for him to decide upon the shrimp with coconut, which he had long ago settled on anyway. He ordered the wine, a Burgundy. A village wine, he told her, shaking his head, as if some shame were on it.

That done, they sat in silence. Having made the effort, having navigated the difficult waters of the menu, steered through its rocky shallows, he'd come up on some escarpment and could rest. His arms were crossed on the table, his face turned down and his thumbs pressing together. Then he turned sideways, as he often did, crossed his legs to the side of the table, and looked through narrowed eyes into the room's smoky distance, as if calculating some danger in the doorway. He was looking in that determined way that made others look too, wondering what he could be staring at so intently. No more should be expected of him. When he looked absorbed in this way, she wondered if his mind's eye were fixed on one of those foreign landscapes or if he were testing out how he would say this or that in his book. She thought not. Those destinations he wrote about, even though carefully described, seemed accidental discoveries, as if he had never given more than a moment's reflection to them.

It was not (it never was) a "companionable" silence. Such silences were, she supposed, rare for anybody. But it would have been nice to sit there in one. She sighed and looked around the restaurant, whose basic color was shell pink. The walls were painted in this pale pink and the woodwork was a cocoa brown. It was a restful color scheme. The napkins were pink, folded intricately into tulip shapes. Music, a flute and piano, floated through the speaker system. Everything was very soothing. It was hard to imagine raising one's voice in such an atmosphere. Green fronds of palms moved slightly when the door opened and shut and cast thin shadows on the pale walls. She felt sleepy; she would have loved to close her eyes.

It would be futile to ask him any more questions about the *tzanta*. Anyway, the subject was awfully morbid. She had pursued it first out of interest, then simply to make him talk. To converse. How could someone so disinclined toward using the language write? The simple explanation would be that his disinclination was toward her and not language. Then why was he so persistent in the matter of these lunches?

The wine arrived and then the appetizers. Often she didn't have one but she'd ordered one today because the pleasant waiter seemed to have so much faith in the onion fritter. Beside it on the small pink plate was a cool, milky-looking mint sauce. It was delicious. He had his mussels, and his absorption in them increased with every mouthful. The act of chewing was for him soporific. His mind was full of mussels.

"How's your fritter?"

SIXTEEN

There was a tree, he'd told her, so poisonous that its very shadow could kill.

The tree fascinated her. She'd wanted more details, but as usual he evaded her questions.

That evening, through her bedroom window overlooking the backyard, she had stared down at the tree near her garage. It was a big maple and dominated the property. It was far enough from the house proper to make a child feel she had escaped and was free of parents and siblings, free of everyone. It was the sort of tree one would climb, hang a swing from, build a tree house in.

Had she done these things as a child? She did not remember.

She had played too long in its shadow, and now that part of her was dead.

It was in the Railway Café the next morning that she thought of this. The waitress was pouring coffee into her cup. The cook had suggested she might like a bacon and egg sandwich instead of an omelet. It was too early for lunch, a little after ten-thirty.

The waitress had returned the Pyrex pot to the burner and was washing glasses behind the counter. She ate her sandwich and wondered who had been using all of this glassware and silver the waitress was washing up. The sandwich was delicious; she could have eaten two. She wondered if it would seem greedy if she told the waitress she wanted another.

As she ate, the ten-thirty-seven pulled in and sat throbbing on the tracks. Through the café window she could make out some of the faces in the passenger car, heavily shadowed. This was also a mail train, so the stationmaster (who always appeared out of nowhere, like a genie) was busy with the mailbags, pushing them somewhere down the platform that she could not see.

The train finally chugged out with no announcement of its arrival or departure, but that happened sometimes when the mail had to be gathered aboard. Now it was quiet enough to hear the tick of the regulator clock on the café's wall.

The door opened then and a father walked in, carrying his child. The little boy was easily old enough to walk alone, but he didn't want to. He wanted to be carried. When the father tried to loosen the grip of the boy's arms from around his neck, the child whimpered and clung more tightly. The father pulled his face back as much as he could to look in the child's face. It was bent down and avoiding the father's eyes. The father talked to him for a moment and the boy nodded reluctantly, released his grip, and slipped down to the floor. With his fingers in his mouth and his head still disconsolately turned downward, the boy permitted the father to sit him in a chair.

She turned from watching the father and child to see that the waitress was putting a dip of chocolate ice cream into a glass and then filling it with soda water. She took this over to the little boy, along with a spoon and a straw. It was clear that the child, even though he didn't speak, even though he kept his head tilted down, was pleased by this. She could see his sly little eyes sliding to the soda, assessing it. But he was not about to give up so easily.

The father pulled his own chair close, put his arm around the back of the boy's chair, and talked to him softly. His voice was so low it was no more than a humming, the vibration of a stringed instrument. The boy would at one point nod, at another shove his face against the father's shoulder. But as he did this, his fingers were moving cunningly toward the soda.

She wondered if the child's mother had departed on the train that had just pulled out, had left them. Temporarily, of course, but to a child it could seem permanent. She was sorry she hadn't got up to see someone actually board the train. For it made the train seem more real, and the station and the café, instead of a story she was telling herself.

The child must have felt betrayed by the world and everyone in it, so he wasn't going to give up easily, chocolate soda or no chocolate soda. She imagined the father had long ago convinced him that his mother was coming back, but the child needed to let it be known how he felt about her leaving. For who knew but what the father would capriciously take it into his head to leave too?

The waitress returned to the table with her order pad. The child hid his face from her, even as he put his fingertips on the glass, as if staking his claim to it, in case she'd come to take the soda away. The father and the waitress smiled over the top of the boy's head, and the man asked for coffee and asked the child what he would like. With his face buried in the wool of his father's jacket he shook his head violently. He could not eat food, not at such a time. And then the father seemed to be making suggestions and the boy finally said something. It sounded like "French fries." The boy did and did not want to look at the waitress. What he really wanted was to look but not to be looked at. Being looked at would draw him into behavior he would much rather avoid. Besides, it would not get him the attention he deserved. It was the same with the soda: he wanted it but could not be seen to want it. This way, neither the soda nor the waitress had any power over him. Neither, in this circumstance, did his father, although he permitted his father to touch him.

But his mother had left him and the world would have to pay. He would drown it in tears, he would punch it and kick it, kick any part of it that he could reach. He would not be consoled. Even though he believed his father when he told the boy his mother would come back, even so that did not give her the right to go off in the first place, leaving him behind. He would not be won over by an ice-cream soda.

Still. . . .

He picked up the straw and hit his father's nose with it, a harmless gesture that allowed him to attack his father — who must be deeply at fault, somehow, in the question of the mother's departure — while at the same time he could draw attention to the straw. The straw was interested in the soda, even if the child was not.

The father stripped the straw of its white tissuelike cover and put it in the glass, saying something to the child as he moved the glass closer. But the boy made quite a show of declining, his head scrubbing back and forth, back and forth against the father's shoulder. No, no, no. No, the child would not reach out his hand, he couldn't be expected to, bad as he felt with the pain of the mother's leaving.

The waitress had brought the father's coffee, but when he started to lift the cup, the child said, "No!" and shoved it back. If the child was too inconsolable to drink his soda, then the father must be too and could hardly drink his coffee. The suspense finally ended when the child (having extracted every morsel of suffering he possibly could from his mother's leaving) finally started drinking his soda — cheerfully, happily

— as if nothing at all had ever happened to make him sad.

She did not know if all or any of this went through the child's mind, but it amused her to make it up and charmed her to think it might be so. What was even more charming was the magnificent patience of the father. He must have understood quite well what the son was feeling and could actually get inside the boy's skin. To have such a parent!

Had she? Her own father had died when she was so small she couldn't remember. And her mother? No. Such a performance would have tried her mother's patience to the breaking point. Sitting here now, looking at the crust of her sandwich, she thought, sadly, that such a performance would never have been undertaken by her five-year-old self, either. For her mother would have reacted coldly, not because she was cruel but because she would have been deeply embarrassed that her child could behave so badly in public. It was a reflection, you see, upon her upbringing, a point against the parent. Her mother believed in appearances — one could say, almost religiously; reality would have meant little or nothing to her mother. She wondered, could that be why she felt unreal so much of the time? Amorphous, formless, a ghost, not there? Either she or the world was. It was as if the world had shrunk to a single dimension. A thing to be watched rather than entered. Was she a patchwork person, made up of odd bits and pieces of others' needs and wants, stitched together in haste?

The child drank his soda, totally immersed in it. She looked out of the window at the edge of the roof, still slowly raining although the rain had stopped, and she could see herself walking through one of those great, empty, windy railway stations — Waterloo, the Gare du Nord — in the early morning or late at night. She could hear her footsteps echo in the booking hall, reverberate up to the enormous vaulted roof. She saw it all as in a Magritte painting: the row of ticket windows, all the same; the faces behind them, all the same; arrivals and departures, all the same.

It was a kind of hell, the place of lost footsteps, and yet she breathed a sigh almost of relief, for it allowed her to abandon such false hopes as she had (and they were few enough) and to give up asking herself the question of why she didn't leave this place. It would make no difference if she did.

When the waitress came to her with the Pyrex pot, she asked, "May I have an ice-cream soda, please? Chocolate."

The waitress nodded and carefully wrote the order down.

It always pleased her, the way the waitress wrote down every request. It lent an air of importance to each order, too important to chance to one's tricky memory, and so she wrote each one down.

At the other table the father was reading the

newspaper. The child, though, must have heard her order the chocolate soda, for he turned around in his chair. He leaned his chin on the back of it, looked to see if he had her attention, and smiled a chocolate smile.

She smiled back. Something in common.

SEVENTEEN

That afternoon they met at the Spanish restaurant, where he said he'd been famished for some paella. Probably because it has mussels in it, she said.

But he would never agree to that, no.

He seldom agreed with anything she said, only conceding a point or two if she were being especially astute, which to his way of thinking she seldom was. He said his hunger for the paella was probably because he wanted to go back to Spain.

She was completely thrown by this. She laughed abruptly and used a bullfighting term to describe him. He was, she said, "cleverly evasive."

This earned her a rare point. Had she not said "cleverly" and said it in Spanish, he would have hotly denied it. But he actually asked her what she meant.

It was indeed as close to outright criticism as she ever got, and even here it was heavily modified. She laughed and said to him, "You field all questions beautifully." She was fully aware that he did not do this beautifully, but stubbornly.

"Questions about what?"

"Traveling, for one thing."

His frown deepened. "Why on earth would I do that?"

She said she didn't know. Anyway, he did do it.

He poured from the pitcher of sangria and told her she was being ridiculous.

She told him that after his trip to Spain he had said next to nothing. He wouldn't talk about it. And he had even seen the running of the bulls.

Again, he told her it was absurd. Travel was what he did, for God's sake! He was a travel writer.

Yes, and if he wrote about it, why didn't he talk about it?

This had only prompted him into his usual defensive sarcasm. Oh, he was *sorry* if he didn't live up to her concept of a good *conversationalist*. And he had made that sideways turn in his chair, inspecting the room and cutting her out as if she had sat down at his table by accident. Then the food arrived and absolved him (that was really the only way she could put it) from further conversation. He was like a monk taking refuge in a priory, walled in and invulnerable.

Her thoughts returned to the café, to the father and child, as she fiddled with her fork, taking up and putting down a forkful of saffron rice. (She had ordered a mélange of some sort of fish and vegetables.) Only nervousness made her eat at all, at least she told herself it was nerves. It wasn't at all; it was a feeling closer to despair, to emptiness. So the simple movement of fork to mouth assuaged this emptiness for a short while. She thought of the little boy in the café. She smiled.

What would happen, she wondered, if she reached over with a breadstick and tapped him on the nose?

WILDERMUTH

EIGHTEEN

It was at lunch a couple of weeks after his queer little speech about beauty when they were eating in his favorite restaurant, the French one with the sommelier, that she was thinking about that other conversation.

For the moment she had set beauty aside; she had not forgotten it. She would bring it up in an oblique way, surprise him into answering sensibly, or at least authentically. She did not know what to be oblique about. Something would come to mind. She closed her eyes. *But in the flesh it is immortal.* She wished she knew what it meant.

"You're leaving — when? In two weeks?"

They had spoken little during the consumption of their main courses; he had replied only to the ministrations of waiter and sommelier. He had ordered a Meursault after a good deal of back-and-forth bantering — or at least it sounded so to her unpracticed ear — with the sommelier. The wine had been very good and so had her fish. He had pronounced the mussel salad excellent. She had never heard of such a thing, except for this place, but made no comment. Chicken with garlic cloves had followed the salad.

The waiters, having nothing to do now, did less. They stood about with their hands folded, occasionally dusting a table with a napkin, adjusting the silver and goblets, commenting about something. The diners, possibly. There appeared to be little to gossip about in this restaurant, empty as it was. It was a little before six o'clock and no one had as yet appeared for dinner, which started, officially, at five-thirty. The couple at the nearby table had departed some time ago. They were the only diners now.

He was in no hurry to finish his *oeufs à la neige,* which she was also eating. The chef could not make the dish for just one person. It was delicious. Rarely did she feel the need to finish up with a sweet; it tended to overpower the mingled tastes, the subtle flavors in her mouth. But this was a dessert her mother used to make when she was a child. She had always thought she could see a blue tint at the bottom of the meringues floating on the custard. Then it was called Floating Island.

"Next week," he replied, to her question about the time of his leaving. "End of the week. Friday, probably."

She felt a small secret shock, and *"Oh"* was all she could manage; she seemed to have breath just for the indrawn syllable. Why this flutter of anxiety? "That soon? Well." She fiddled with her dessert spoon. "Will you have time for lunch, then, next week?"

"Oh, I expect so." He was expansive, having finished the excellent custard. He lighted a cigar and now blew a smoke ring. He seemed almost indifferent to the dangers of such a trip.

"Bolivia. Imagine."

But wasn't *imagine* just what he could *not* do? Was he actually fearless, or did he simply lack imagination? All of these places he went to, or would be going to. Exotic, romantic, or dangerous to ordinary people, for whom they were not so much actual places as rumors of places.

"You take it all so calmly. You're so sanguine. How can you be? Don't you feel at all anxious?" She leaned toward him in her intense desire to know.

He frowned and studied the lighted end of his cigar. He did not respond; she was used to that, but this failure to reply seemed different. She had set her foot over some fine line, tripped over it, really, into territory where she had no business to be. At least, she imagined this to be true. *Why are you asking this wasn't part of the bargain my feelings are not part of the bargain.* What bargain? He spread his hands as if to take in the lunch, the restaurant, themselves. The whole unexplored terrain. *Savages, the humid dark, the wading birds, the impenetrable green jungle, morning mist rising from the river like a god.* She saw this.

But his hand moved only to pluck up the globe enclosing the candle and blow out the flame. He signaled the waiter.

It was as if, in slipping, she had crossed the border to some other country in which irony and mockery were no longer sanctioned.

He smoked his cigar and watched one of the waiters smoothing a tablecloth, reshaping a napkin into one of those intricate shapes that she had always thought indicated more attention paid to the trappings of a meal than to the meal itself, a showy ambience that masked a kind of failure.

Their own waiter had brought the check and collected the credit card and gone off.

"I only mean," she said, recasting the question as a statement, "you're so easy about it all."

"Um. I'm used to it, that's all." He rolled the cigar in his mouth and looked over her shoulder, out the window.

Was this detachment a kind of punishment for her getting personal? But what in God's name was personal about asking why he took the up-coming trip so calmly? He had, after all, stepped into *her* encampment by telling her she spent too much time in the café. And what was so different between a trip to Bolivia and her station café? She laughed.

"What's so funny?" He looked up from the voucher he'd been signing.

"Oh, nothing. I was just thinking, when it comes down to it, how alike we are."

"No," he said, ripping the receipt from the voucher. "We aren't."

NINETEEN

This went through her mind the following week as the waitress crossed the room and spoke to her. What the waitress said was, "Cook's out this morning. So it's me who'll have to do the omelet, I mean if that's what you're planning on having," she added, as if not wanting to seem too familiar. "I know how he does it, I've watched. But that doesn't mean I'd do it right. Maybe you'd rather have something else?"

It was jarring to her. Had she been superstitious or a believer in prophecy, this interruption of normal routine following on the heels of last week's lunch would have made her apprehensive. Lunch had caused a tremor, a quake, hardly noticeable except for the fissure at the bottom of the structure. A wall beginning to crumble.

"Will he be back?" The question came, unbidden.

"Pretty soon, he will." The waitress looked at her small wristwatch as if to confirm this. "He only just went down to the courthouse." Here she rolled her eyes. "And you know how long *that* takes!"

She smiled at the waitress and nodded, though she had never once been to the courthouse.

But the waitress was treating all this with a sort of gravity, as if the loss of the cook for the morning were not to be taken lightly. She stood calmly before the table, her pencil poised over her tablet of checks. "What I *can* make is French toast. The best, if I do say it."

"Yes. That sounds good. I love French toast."

French toast was written down on her pad. Then the waitress said, "How about some sausage with that? We get it from Seabold's, that farm out on One-eleven."

She knew nothing about Seabold's farm but smiled and nodded, as if the sausage must be guaranteed if it came from Seabold's. "Yes."

The waitress wrote that down, too, and also coffee. "Okay. It'll be fifteen, maybe twenty minutes." She put the tablet in her uniform pocket and went off.

She sat there and looked at the door to the kitchen the waitress had just gone through. It was still swinging gently.

With the disappearance of the waitress, she was now alone in the room. Only once or twice before had she noticed the light ticking of the regulator clock. If she were alone where she hadn't been alone before, were noises then going to take on this knife-edged clarity?

She took out her book, the one she carried around for waiting reading. Waiting in a line at the supermarket or in the post office. Waiting for a meal to be served. Sometimes during the meal. She loved to read while she ate, but supposed it was bad both for the mind and the body. One should not need to be distracted to this degree. At least, she didn't turn on the television, as some people did, for company. The book was a mystery, and already after only thirty or forty pages she was bored with it. It had a cadaverous feel to it — bloodless, the prose stale and lifeless, no hearts in these characters to pump blood through their veins and out onto the sheet of paper. How strange, she thought. By page forty, three people had been murdered in an especially gory fashion, and the characters reacted as if someone had simply been swatting flies. Back went the book into her bag. She pulled over the little bottle that held flowers and wondered about mystery writers. Were they all, in part, despicable? Probably. She touched the delicate petals of the blue acanthus. Yes, probably. Perfectly nice people in the main, but there was that one cringing place in their souls that provoked them toward this sort of writing, writing that hated to show its hand and would only go in directions where the rules were firmly established and could, in some ironic sense, serve as wild cards that could be played any which way. In the beginning of such books, events appeared accidental and confused, but as the story lumbered on, solutions started occurring, and by the end everything was the opposite of accidental and confused; it was all neatly tied up.

Somehow comforted and refreshed by these observations about mysteries and those who wrote them (although she bore these people no malice), she sat back.

She had thought her life accidental; now she saw it was arranged: the same things done at the same times with scarcely any room for accident. She closed her eyes and dreamed a ballet. Her life as a series of carefully executed steps. But it was probably more like a chessboard, where queen and king and rooks and pawns moved by stringent rules. Perhaps like the chessboard in *Alice in Wonderland*. Except those pieces kept changing the rules to suit themselves, didn't they? The Red Queen certainly had.

Unconsoled, she felt as thin as vapor. Her routine — café, lunch with her friend, afternoon at the library twice a week — had gone on for many months and she had been content in it. Or, at least, accepting of it. To others, her life would appear mean, meager.

Only now there was this feeling of alarm. Was it caused simply by the cook's not being there?

Why not? Why must she regard the cook's absence as of no importance? Great events, governments toppling, the heroine's flight into madness — weren't they all occasioned by the cook's not being there? Wasn't it only in books like those mystery stories that cause and effect were discernible and, after having been discovered, were obvious? The cook, in such stories, was always there.

So she could not compare her life to a story, and not to a ballet. It wasn't like gracefully executed steps but a jumble of trembling movements, unchoreographed and unrehearsed. Anything could happen within the boundaries of these repeated events. Or was it possible that the cook's absence was caused by the fumbling question put to her friend: *Why?* Was this what scientists called the butterfly effect? The butterfly in China moved its wings and caused an earthquake in California?

The waitress was back now, placing the French toast before her and the small oval dish of sausage patties. She was surprised that she was starving hungry. But she did not want to eat too much, for she was meeting her friend at three o'clock. Well, it was only ten now; she would be hungry again in five hours. But if the cook had been here, this French toast and sausage would not have happened and the waitress would not be speaking to her again.

"Thing is, once you start, it just becomes habit, doesn't it?" The waitress said this as if picking up the threads of an old conversation, interrupted. "And habits you get into are hard to break. You know what I mean?" She said this thoughtfully while setting the little schooner of maple syrup onto a saucer. A ribbon of thick syrup was already running down the side. "Like this waiting tables —"

Afraid the waitress was about to launch into an accounting of some part of her life, she asked quickly, "What happened to the cook? Why did he go to the courthouse?" And then she remembered, too late, it might be dangerous to ask why. Still, this was the cook, and she was only asking to be told a fact.

"Ticket," said the waitress cheerfully, apparently not bothered by having her own opinions cut off. "Speeding ticket, and he's going to contest it. He claims he was within the speed limit, that the trooper was wrong. I know he's a careful driver, I've driven with him. He's going to contest it," she repeated. The waitress was obviously pleased by this. "Of course, he doesn't stand a chance, going up against the law."

And she seemed even more pleased by this — that the cook would have the courage to go up against the weight of the police force in a losing battle. Which is what she said: "A losing battle, I suppose." Then turning toward the window, she added, "We should fight more of them." With that rather opaque comment, the waitress walked away.

As she ate her French toast, which was exceedingly tasty, she wondered: if it were the waitress who'd got the speeding ticket, would the cook have shown the same concern for her? Yes, she thought, he would. Would the cook have said that she, the waitress, had courage? That she wouldn't lie down and let the authorities walk all over her?

But if one wasn't aware of the danger (as the cook clearly had been), could one call it courage? She thought not.

The waitress was back at her post at the end of the counter, looking out of the window, smoking. A flare of sunlight opened like a fan across the glass and lit her apron as if it were white flame.

She chewed her sausage and wondered if people could perform courageous acts without realizing it. She frowned. But wouldn't that be the same as not realizing the danger involved? She drank her coffee and wondered if she herself had courage. Looking back even to her childhood she searched for anything she had done that might be called courageous and could remember nothing. No, but there was one instance when she was a child of eight or nine and had taken the blame for a friend named Sissy. She could not actually recall what Sissy had done, only that Sissy had been frightened for having done it. Her mother would smack her. Had Sissy broken something? Ruined something? For the life of her she couldn't remember. At any rate, she did remember the hard and angry face of Sissy's mother. So she had said that she alone had done it, that Sissy wasn't to blame, and, of course, Sissy's mother did not feel free to smack *her;* mothers could not go around smacking other people's children.

Then why could she call her act courageous? For she wasn't in any danger of being smacked.

Yet there must be courage of another kind, surely. Courage that had little to do with threats of violence against one. And then she thought that no particular act was in itself courageous. A glide down the snowy hill behind the courthouse building would hardly be courageous for an Olympic skier. But for a novice, it might well take courage. Then it was relative, like beauty. An eight-year-old could not analyze the danger as an adult could. A child could look into a face blazing with anger and know the anger was there, and meant for the child, whether or not the child was struck. So, yes, it had taken courage. She felt somewhat relieved. But now she wondered about that lunch last week and whether she had known on some level that her question (and how innocent a question!) would come dangerously close to upsetting the balance. Of what, she did not know.

She was frightened that she had turned the screw a notch too far and disturbed an equilibrium. That she hadn't realized how carefully the scales were balanced. From sanity to madness was a hair's-breadth turn. Because (she imagined) there was very little difference between the end of one and the beginning of the other.

Beneath her feet the faint tremor of the floor told her the ten-thirty-seven was coming in. Another of those portents in advance of an earthquake. It was a passenger train and she ordinarily was on the platform at this time, if she was at the station, for she enjoyed looking into the train windows at the faces of the passengers, sleepy, bored, bent over books and newspapers.

But she hadn't finished her breakfast, so she

merely observed what she could through the window of the café. It wasn't much, just the loading of a few large crates. No one got off, no one got on, from what she could see.

She finished her breakfast and sat awhile watching the waitress, who had moved closer to the window and stood looking out at the platform. The train lurched forward once, and then again, trying to gather speed, and finally moved off. The waitress went back to the counter and stood there, hands in pockets, still looking out at the tracks, empty again. The waitress often looked pensive, she thought. *Pensive* was a word she had never used to describe anyone before, but it fit the waitress.

Then the café door opened and a tall, handsome woman dressed in black came in. Without looking around, she sat down at a table for four in the corner. Her air of assurance, her manner, her clothes spoke of someone used to money and, being used to it, someone who did not have to ask for service or wait for it. She had been carrying one of those small bags referred to as a *train case,* a boxlike affair of rich brown alligator skin with a handle on top, which she now positioned on the chair beside her. Then she sat and plucked the menu from between the sugar bowl and the napkin holder. Her plain black suit had a long skirt, nearly to the ankle, with a kick pleat. A beautiful cut made up for whatever the suit lacked by way of ornament. She wore no jewelry, which was surprising, dressed up as she was in this suit and a small black hat. Yet, the lack of jewelry further suggested an aplomb, a self-possession that did not need to be set off by gold or diamonds.

The waitress moved over to the table as soon as the woman sat down; she was giving an order for something, probably coffee, for she had barely looked at the menu before wedging it back.

It was good to see another woman eating alone, traveling alone. To know she wasn't the only one. She felt a kinship with the woman in black, despite the latter's elegance. But perhaps the woman in black was no more intelligent than she herself. She would have liked to pose the question about beauty to this woman, whose eyes, as she looked around the room, seemed ruminative, speculative. A time or two she looked back over her shoulder, toward the door.

And in another few moments, a man walked through and put an end to any notion of this woman's being alone. The waitress was carrying coffee and some sort of pastry to the table and the man was calling for coffee too.

Of course, it had been ridiculous of her to think that this woman would be on her own. A woman who looked and acted like that.

The man was equally well dressed. The coat he had tossed over the back of the chair was cashmere, the color of hot sand.

She wondered where they were going. Or, rather, where the woman was going, for the man struck her, for some reason, as the person staying behind. Perhaps that was only because he carried no bag.

The waitress returned almost immediately with his coffee and the Pyrex pot to refill the woman's cup. After she left the table, they settled into a comfortable intimacy, drinking their coffee and eating pastry.

The cook came back.

He nodded to the man and woman in the corner, who didn't see him or didn't care.

He nodded and also smiled at her, giving the impression that she was one of the stable fixtures in the café. She appreciated that and returned his smile. His face was flushed and his eyes were bright, as if he'd been drinking champagne. Indeed, he was so elated that he hugged the waitress, who laughed. He must have won his case over the speeding ticket and now he was recounting it to the waitress.

At the corner table the man and woman were gathering themselves together, their coats and her bag, preparatory to leaving. The man turned in his chair and signaled the waitress. But the waitress paid no attention; the hand waving in air probably hadn't even registered on her consciousness, for she was attending only to the cook's return and his story.

The cook was gesticulating, throwing his arms about, but keeping his voice low enough that all she heard was a murmur. She was glad that he'd won; it seemed important to her that he should, although she was not sure why.

Now the man and woman were standing at the corner table. He was clearly irritated because he could not get the waitress to attend to him. She was laughing at the cook's story. Finally, the man walked over to them, his face set in hard lines. Incensed, he announced that the waitress was keeping them waiting. Then his voice dropped and she could hear only words here and there.

But she could see the waitress's mouth tighten. The cook shoved his expressive hands in his trouser pockets and turned away, toward the kitchen: he stopped at the door, though, to look back.

He was wondering, perhaps, what he should do. There was of course no threat implied by the man's words, only bad temper. The man spread his arms and looked around him, and at her, sitting alone, as if including the entire café in his sense of the waitress's disregard for the customers. It was inexcusable since there was but one other table occupied. He pointed as he said, "Only her," incorporating her in his argument, making her an ally. This made her angry, his sweeping her into his complaint, almost making her a party to it.

The woman in black had stood and continued to stand at their table, her smooth pale face revealing nothing, her thoughts a mystery. Perhaps she too was irritated with the waitress, her rich life having been peopled with servants who came swiftly at her beck and call. Or perhaps she thought he was being a boor. She was unreadable.

Now the man was silent and stiff as a statue, waiting for his change. The old cash register, an antique, had a cash drawer that slapped open with a *shring!* The waitress started making change but was having trouble. The cook was still at the door to the kitchen and walked over behind the counter. She said something to the cook; he nodded and took the money and walked out of the café.

What she understood from their discussion was that the man had given the waitress a hundred-dollar bill. For a check that had probably been three dollars at most. She thought this man often created scenes like this one, doing himself no good in the process. For she bet he had a few loose dollars in his money clip and was using the hundred-dollar bill to be difficult and ostentatious. The result was that now he would have to wait again until the cook could go somewhere outside the station, over to the bank, perhaps. She thought about the cook. She wondered what inner resources he had that would permit him to stand up to the police, the judge, the system. She was quite sure she could not have done this herself. She would simply have paid the ticket. Yet, that did not disturb her, for she was sure most people would have done the same thing.

The man remained at the counter, sighing his disapproval, glaring at the door through which the cook had left, paying no attention at all to the woman in black, still standing beside their table, her hand on the train case.

It was infuriating that one person could thrust his bad temper onto the entire room, plaguing them all, infecting them with his anger. She despised the man and his transaction, for he had ruined the cook's moment of victory.

TWENTY

This was the last lunch they would eat until he came back from La Paz and the river. Not the Amazon, the other one. She couldn't remember the name.

The restaurant he had picked this time was German, cramped and a little dingy but full of rich and redolent odors.

She was having soup as a first course; he was eating steamed mussels. She was surprised to see mussels on the menu of a German restaurant. Probably the chief reason he'd chosen the place.

The soup was a heavy concoction that included dumplings, a whole meal in itself. After her late French-toast breakfast, she was going to have a hard time getting all of her lunch down. She wouldn't have ordered soup, except the waiter had described this one as a broth and she had assumed it would be no heavier than a consommé. The Germans must have an odd notion of what a broth is, she thought. For her main course, she had ordered herring salad, hoping that would be a light dish.

He had ordered something elaborate, half a

paragraph on the menu listing its contents, of which she could make out several kinds of sausage — bratwurst among others — potato salad, or possibly pancakes, spätzle, red cabbage. . . .

When he ordered in German, she was not surprised. She supposed he spoke the languages of most of the countries he'd been to. Fluently, too, for he had discussed the wine with the waiter. So delighted was the waiter to have a patron who not only knew something about wine but who also spoke the language, he led him on a tour of the wine list. They laughed several times, joking in German. They settled on a Chardonnay. The language she found solid and heavy, like the food, blunt and lacking grace — lacking the trill of Spanish, the lovely sliding sounds of French.

German, French, Spanish. He talked as little about languages as he did about his travels. "That's the third language, outside of English, I've heard you speak." She smiled.

His head was, of course, bent over his bowl of mussels. He shrugged her comment off. "You pick it up when you do all of the traveling I do."

"No, it's not just picked up. Your fluency is much greater than you'd get from standing around the water pump with a couple of natives." When he simply grunted and poked at another shell, she decided not to ask him what other languages he knew. She wondered if a truly stupid question would prise his eyes up from the mussels. "What do they speak in La Paz? Bolivian?" She had meant to make a joke.

The head stayed down. In all seriousness he answered, "No. Spanish."

They continued to eat in silence, he in his "bolting" posture, the chair pushed back so that he could turn his legs to the side and cross them, his torso also turned slightly, one shoulder in. Head down. Had she imagined it all — his discomfort, his hidden anger at her questions? For he seemed exactly the same. She wasn't sure whether she was relieved or only further irritated by his obtuseness. Perhaps she was assigning him levels of selfhood that he had no awareness of, even levels he didn't truly have. Or perhaps she was projecting her own uncertainties onto him. Her own fears.

She tried to imagine herself walking into such a situation as the one he was soon to face. Packing up, locking her door. Waiting on the station platform for a train now *her* train. Hearing the announcement: *The train now departing on Track One for La Paz* — a winged train, a train like a hovercraft riding inches above the water. She would be one of the faces on the other side of the windows, staring out at the platform and the empty air she had recently occupied. . . . Such a maneuver to her would be apocalyptic. Didn't he see that?

She looked at the spoonful of soup, trembling in the bowl, an odd brownish-yellow. She thought of his river. Mud-bottomed, a thick, slow movement of brown. Not the steely gray clarity of crystal that we attach to rivers, sliding and percolating around gray rock. . . .

"How's your soup?"

Her eyes snapped open. She hadn't realized they'd been partly shut until this, the inevitable question. She looked across at the neat stack of mussel shells. He was plying the tiny fork at one still in its shell.

"All right." She paused. "I was thinking of the river."

He did not answer.

She was sure he had not heard. So she said it again. "The river."

His eyes jerked upward, eyebrows raised, surprised at this intrusion of thought into his mussels.

"I was thinking that if it were me, I'd be afraid. Afraid," she said again.

He cleared his throat. "Oh, I don't know." Taking refuge in the group of waiters talking together at the back of the room, he signaled theirs.

Her smile was a bit shaky as she said, *"You* don't know. I *do."*

"Finished your soup, haven't you?" He was inspecting the condiments, the horseradish, the mustard pot.

"Yes." Determined, she went on. *"I'd* be afraid to go down that river. Through that jungle."

"Oh? Why's tha— ? Blast it!" The mustard pot slipped from his fingers, knocking on the table edge on its way to the floor, where it spun, unbroken. He was under the table in a flash, scooping it up. He laughed shortly, replaced the

125

pot on the table. "Tough jar. Germans know how to make things. In Essen, I remember this restaurant where there was mustard. . . ."

He was off on some obscure tale about mustard and Essen that wouldn't have interested anyone even if it had been the last printed page in the world. She felt hopeless, then angry, which was more productive. He carried on this painful *longueur* until the waiter came with herring and bratwurst, providing respite from Essen and mustard.

She decided she would have to race him to the next interruption, which was the wine's being poured, and referred to the book, making her reading of it seem accidental. "I came across a reference to this river in the library. Apparently, it runs through one of the wildest terrains in the world, and traveling down it is like reentering the Pleistocene Age."

He wasn't looking at her, of course. He was cutting his bratwurst into neat thick coins.

"The natives have no commerce with the civilized world. *Savages* is what the book called them, and all along its length are some of the most dangerous reptiles that exist." She had not read this but had begun now to make things up. "Crocodiles, copperheads, water moccasins. To say nothing of the savages." Could she scare him into a meaningful response? Must it be torn, ripped from him? He would have to be desperate. Nothing short of his clawing at air, screaming for help, watching the wet blade drawn from his entrails would do it.

Eyes on his plate, he said, "How's your herring?"

Her face hot, feeling the drumbeat of her own blood, she thought of wreaking havoc as she quietly ate her dinner. She thought of the woman in black, cold and smooth as an ivory moon far from a source of heat, and she felt a kinship with her. One becomes that way; one has to. What had driven that woman to retreat behind that mask was probably the man and his impossible demands.

"That passage is from 'Peter Quince at the Clavier,' " she said.

He looked up, innocently puzzled. "What's that? What passage?"

" 'Beauty is momentary in the mind.' The one you quoted. It's from 'Peter Quince.' "

His brow furrowed, and he looked off into the shadowy darkness of the restaurant.

It might have been bright light outside, but in here it became harder to see beyond the crescent rim of candlelight on their table. Or so it affected her.

"That *I* quoted?"

Oh, he was surely not this cheap; he was not simply going to *deny* he'd done so? "Yes, you'd forgotten the second line, though. Or part of it."

"Ah!" He breathed this out as if the point, long contested, were now settled.

" 'The fitful tracing of a portal.' I've been wondering about the meaning of that line. And the other."

He tried on his contemplative look for the few moments he could tear his eyes away from his plate. "Um-hm." Now he was eating red cabbage. He pointed his fork at it. "Delicious. This place is a real find. Yes, quite a find."

She wasn't going to stop. "It was the idea of relative beauty that you brought up. *You* brought it up." She wanted to add *all by yourself, I was amazed.* "You said Tahiti was 'relatively beautiful.' In relation to, relative to Maui, it wasn't all that beautiful, and you quoted Wallace Stevens. 'Beauty is momentary —' "

Now he was chuckling. "You're really obsessed with Maui and Tahiti." He shook his head in wonder at her obsession. "You should go there, you know."

"I don't want to go there. They're merely examples."

"Umm." He spooned sour cream over a pancake.

"Examples of *your* notion of relative beauty." When he made no response, not even a grunt, she asked (too desperately), "Are you even *listening?*" This was the wrong approach; this would allow him to derail any semblance of reasonable conversation.

"Every *word.* I'm *sorry* if you think I'm paying no *attention,* but I was merely trying to enjoy my *dinner.* I wasn't aware that we'd come out to lunch together so that we could have a *running* conversation — now let's *see* . . . what would you like to talk about?" He looked at her with severity, as if she were indeed showing signs of ob-session, of a craziness that would bring the waiters running.

But she was not going to let him get out of this by mocking her. It was one of his favorite ruses. " 'Beauty is momentary in the mind' — *that's* what we'll talk about."

It was as if she hadn't spoken. But then she knew she was invisible, didn't she?

Buttering another slice of thick black bread, he said, "Did you know that crocodiles can't look back?"

So alarming was this question in its irrele-vance, it left her speechless.

"It's true. Did you ever *see* one looking over its shoulder?" he asked, with his astonishing sanguineness, and as if she'd denied the truth of it. "Crocodiles can't turn their heads to look back. I suppose the best thing to do is to make sure you're standing behind them."

She abandoned Wallace Stevens to say, "Back-ward or forward, crocodiles are dangerous." Then she asked, point-blank, "Don't you ever feel in danger?"

"Hmm. Oh, occasionally. I expect we all do, don't we?" He speared a sausage and popped it into this mouth, chewed, let his eyes rove the shadowy room, refuse to rest on her, even for a moment.

"No. *Not* all. I'm talking about dangers you've met in your travels. Have you ever felt in danger anywhere?"

He was finishing off his bratwurst and the cabbage. Probably he wouldn't answer. But he did. "I think I must have in Tibet. Climbing. Mountain climbing, I mean."

She had no idea he'd been to Tibet. That pulled her, an involuntary movement, forward in her chair. "Tibet?"

"They didn't want to take me, of course — the crew didn't. No experience. Can hardly blame them." The last of the potato pancake disappeared into his mouth.

He talked of it as if it had been a walk around the block. It was she who stopped listening, this time. She visualized mountains, cliffs, canyons with sheer faces. Red rocks rising out of a desolate landscape. Unpeopled places, lonely beyond imagining.

". . . the cortege dragging the *polizia* in their wake." He chuckled again.

"What? What police?"

He waggled his knife at her. "Aren't you even listening?"

"Was this in Venice?" She remembered he had spent a couple of months there.

"This funeral. Well, of course they go to the cemetery in boats, don't they? Gondolas painted black . . . it's quite impressive to watch them. My friend — it was his motorboat, not mine — dared me to join the funeral cortege. Which I promptly did. Having drunk two bottles of rather excruciating wine. So there I was in the middle of the mourners' black boats —" He had to stop to laugh.

She stared. That was like him, wasn't it? Making a mockery of the funeral procession. Rutting the waves in his toy boat, probably with flags flying. Gondolas like black swans drifting. She wondered who had died. " 'Death in Venice,' " she said, suddenly and sadly.

"Ah, yes. What was his name? Aren— ?"

"Aschenbach." She said it sadly. "There was the plague, then. He couldn't leave, he was under a spell, mesmerized."

Beauty is momentary in the mind.

"Was the family . . . immune?" She frowned over the word. "Was he immune, the boy who was so beautiful? Like one of those mythological figures, or the sort of person the Pre-Raphaelites liked to paint. He was untouched by the plague. Aschenbach died of it. Did the boy's beauty make him immune?"

"You read too many books."

She started. He was not so stupid that he would make such a foolish statement; he did it because he enjoyed mouthing absurdities at her.

"I read too few."

Now he was looking over his shoulder for the waiter, who had disappeared. "Where in hell do they get to? Why is one never around when you want him?"

"Like the *polizia*," she said, smiling. She was going along with him.

"Yes." He laughed. *"Polizia."*

She was going along and in some part of his mind he knew it, though he wouldn't or couldn't verbalize it. After all, this was the last lunch until he came back from Bolivia. And, really, why did she think she was the one to be setting the tone? Establishing where the border of intimacy began? Deciding the exchange rate of conversation? They did not even share the same currency; she was from another country and possibly an even poorer one.

When the waiter finally turned up with their coffee, she was thinking that when he came back from his trip she might be more tolerant.

TWENTY-ONE

But he did not come back.

At three or four o'clock every day she would visit one or the other of the restaurants and search the room, take in the faces of the few diners there, and sometimes sit down to eat, although she was never hungry. It was superstitious eating, almost, as if the routine of lunching at a late hour would bring him back.

After two weeks she started questioning the maître d's, the waiters. Did they remember him? Had they seen him? In a few cases, the waiter would recall both of them and tell her no, her friend hadn't been around lately. In the French restaurant, the sommelier remembered him clearly because he had been knowledgeable about wines and even knew certain vineyards in Burgundy, such as Montrachet. Oh, yes, the waiter remembered him well.

In the process of this search, she felt again and again the awful poverty of a friendship of which, despite its having gone on for over a year — all of those lunches! — no proof existed except for a telephone number and a few inscribed books.

They had no mutual friend or acquaintance, and she had no mental image of the place where he'd lived (she had never been there), or the room in which he wrote all morning and part of the afternoon. There was only the telephone number and the ghostly voice on the answering machine. A month passed in this way, and she still had no clue as to his whereabouts.

Finally, she called his publisher.

She should have thought of it before, as much of their conversation had been about the vicissitudes of the publishing business, about his editor or copy editor. Yet, he had spoken no names, so she did not know whom to ask for.

She told the receptionist who answered (and who was impatient because she'd have to search for the person) that she had no idea of the name of the editor, or anyone there, but they must surely have certain ones who deal with travel.

When she was put through to the second person, she felt she was making progress, for this one said, Yes, she certainly knew the name and would put her through to the editor. It wasn't the editor she got, but his assistant. This young woman seemed hesitant to answer questions about their writers. But she convinced the girl that she was a very good friend and made up some little tale to explain why she had to call the publisher.

"But if you're such a good friend? . . . You don't know?" said the assistant editor. "You hadn't heard he's dead?"

She shut her eyes. She could hardly breathe. Her chest felt tight, as if a fist had clamped her and squeezed, the sort of pain associated with a coronary. But she knew that wasn't its source. She could say nothing into the phone except, "What? What did you say?"

"It happened in — he was killed in the Amazon."

She had to hang up; she couldn't stand to listen to any details right now. She had the receiver halfway to the cradle before she remembered to ask, "When?"

"A month ago. It was the day before he was to come back. . . . But I'm surprised you didn't *hear.*" The girl's voice seemed to be accusing her of a dereliction of friendship. "It was in all the papers."

"I've been — out of the country." She kept feeling she must apologize for her ignorance.

"Well, it was on the news just about everywhere. You must not have known him all that well."

The words were little blows, tiny punishing hammers. She could have died from the shame of not having known.

"What happened was —"

Hurriedly, she thanked the editor's assistant. "I'll call his — family." She had very nearly said "mother" before she realized his mother might be dead.

It was horrible for her that this rather rude girl

was in possession of these details, that she knew if his mother was alive, knew if he had a brother or a sister, knew when and where he was born.

She lowered her forehead to the cool surface of the receiver. Her face felt hot. To think she had been such a peripheral person in his life she had had to hear from a perfect stranger that he was dead one whole month after it had happened.

Certainly, she wanted to know how he'd died (*killed,* hadn't the girl said?) and the details of where and how this had happened, but it would be less painful to read it in a newspaper than to hear it from that swaggering girl, so full of her own importance, working in the reflected light of all of those writers.

She raised her head and wiped her eyes, surprised to find she had been weeping. *It was in all the papers.* Theirs was not a very big town, yet, since he had lived here, the notice should be in the local paper. She would find back issues at the library and, since it had been a month ago, she would not have to look through many of them.

The write-up surprised her, at first by its very length, then by the discovery that he was well known for these travel books, if not absolutely famous for them. She discovered too that his parents were dead and that he had a sister living out west. But none of this had surprised her as much as the circumstances of his death. At first she thought it surely must be a joke, some sort of black humor. In the jungle, he had been mauled by a jaguar. This was hard enough to grasp and made her draw in her breath so quickly she felt the return of the choking pain. But the rest of it was unbelievable. She remembered his talking about a kind of cactus that if cut and the pulp removed and eaten would cause the sort of hallucinations Castaneda had written about. It wasn't peyote; it was something else.

> . . . But, horrible as it must have been, he might have been dead by the time the jaguar leapt, for the pathologist found traces of strychnine in his bloodstream. Police deduced that he had been eating the flesh of the San Pedro cactus, which causes hallucinations, and had not realized that part of this cactus contains strychnine.

She looked up and out over waves of shelved books, watching them tilt, feeling seasick. Strychnine. Hallucinations. Jaguar.

To *him?*

TWENTY-TWO

But what they didn't know — the reporters, the editor's assistant, the editor himself; very possibly, what no one knew except she herself — was the awful irony of it.

Had she not felt so sunk, she would have laughed, laughed herself sick, really. It was the whole drama of his death. The horrific Hollywood-style melodrama of it. The fitting final scene of his meeting his destiny: that's how the movies would have handled it. Well, really, that's how the people at his publishing house were handling it, wasn't it? An interview with his editor had that man saying, *A fitting death for a man who, in a sense, lived to travel.*

He who had despised travel! But wouldn't admit it, or couldn't see it. He who had made trips to those lone and lost places on the globe, so remote from such people as herself that she couldn't even dream of it, such stories he could have told as would have made a Scheherazade of him (and perhaps he had been to his readers). Yet he had remained untouched by these places. He had returned, virginal, from such trips, unseduced and left unconsummated. Travel bored him. Had he been able to report to her his own manner of dying he would probably have called it something like an "odd little circumstance."

Travel bored him, and yet the boredom did not break the gait of his writing. It was as if another part of himself gathered in the reins at that point and wrote about what he'd seen, as if he'd had beside him all that trip a traveling muse who'd found things astounding and delightful and gorgeous. But to *him,* the true him, it was all rather an evening's stroll. Zimbabwe. Puligny-Montrachet. Odessa. Aix-en-Provence. The Amazon. Little to choose between them, except, perhaps, for the wine.

It had not been as interesting to him as the lunches with her had been. She was astonished by her certainty of this. This knowledge somehow redeemed her from the awful ignorance of his death.

Late afternoon. She had come to the station café after leaving the library to have coffee. To sit, really. She could not eat, not even one of the cook's omelets. Unusual for her to be here at this time of day. The stationmaster was announcing the four-fifty, soon to arrive. The waitress and the cook stood together, as usual, at the end of the counter, smoking.

It is perhaps fitting that his death was as dramatic as his life had been.

That had been written about him, in a lengthy obituary, saying again what his editor had said. She held a paper napkin to her mouth. Her shoulders heaved, mixing a laugh and a sob. The sound tore the silence of the café as if it were smashing a windowpane.

The waitress's head turned quickly to look toward her; the cook's cigarette stopped in midair. As of a single mind, they both moved, she toward the coffeepots, he toward the kitchen. He went in and was out in a moment, holding a glass and a bottle. It was brandy, and he was pouring out a small amount and placing it before her while the waitress refilled her empty cup.

Their concern prompted her to say, "My friend died." And this of course was true, but only the truth's bare bones.

Yet, there must be simple statements such as this so that all of them could survive, mustn't there? There had to be some universal code that anyone could crack, that anyone could understand, no matter how much it left out of the complexity of the feelings, the nuances that would be lost on them, the sense of the shadowy, cobwebbed atmosphere in which the friendship had taken place.

She said, "I thought I was — immune." And wept again.

The cook put his hand on her shoulder. The waitress bent to offer a napkin as handkerchief.

Immune. Like the beautiful boy in "Death in

Venice" who had remained untouched by the plague, while Aschenbach sat dying his awful death by the sunstruck sea.

WHEN
THE MOUSETRAP
CLOSES

ONE

1

Edith looked across Mrs. Dawson's Tearoom at the youngish man sitting by himself, reading the newspaper. She looked away, frowned, looked back again. It couldn't be he, surely . . . ? Still, if he took off the glasses —

As if he'd read her mind like a stage direction, he did just that, removed the unflattering horn-rims, held them out to the light, and examined them for smudges.

It *was* Archie Marchbanks. Edith could scarcely believe it. It was Marchbanks, or his twin, sitting at the table by the window, polishing his glasses with his napkin. He was not looking up or around in the manner of a person impressed by his own celebrity.

Edith saw this with only the quickest of glances. Even so, she thought she could have stared at him right over the pastry trolley and he would not have noticed. The gesture of raising the glasses was uncannily like the gesture of the character he'd played with such stunning success in one of the West End theaters last year. Only there the object being examined — it was in the second act — was a diamond-and-ruby necklace. Just that reach of the arm, just that slight squint, that inclination of the head. It was that character to the core.

She had seen the play three times in its last month and was sorry she'd waited so long, for it had been running a good six months when Marchbanks had left it. Another actor had taken his place and the play had closed with what must have been embarrassing swiftness for him. The only thing that had kept the lackluster play alive had been Archie Marchbanks. From the time Marchbanks walked on the stage, she could sense the current in the air. He had been utterly convincing playing the role of a man twice his age. It amazed her that whoever was in charge of casting — casting directors, was that what they were called? — had had the intuition or prescience to give the part to Marchbanks. He was too young, too handsome, too — everything, on the face of it.

Edith looked around the small room, at the occupants of four other tables, one right next to Marchbanks. No one else had recognized him.

2

Edith was a regular customer at Mrs. Dawson's, as she lived nearby in one of the crescents that branched off from the Fulham Road. She was but a short bus ride away from the Victoria and Albert, and she chided herself for not visiting it often enough — scarcely ever, she had to admit. The same carelessness was shown toward the Brompton Oratory. She'd been in it perhaps three or four times since she had made the move to her present flat, which she had shared with her mother until her death two years ago.

It was almost embarrassing to her, the fondness she had always felt for her mother. Edith seemed to measure time by her death; things had happened either before or after the death of Mrs. Parenger. Everyone else she had known carried a mixed bag of emotions around, a deadweight, a steamer trunk packed with feelings for their parents. Any one of these friends would have analyzed her feelings for her mother, presumptively. That was when Mrs. Parenger was alive; they daren't do it now she was dead. Her friend Zoe saw Edith's feelings as *repressed*. "One only has to look at the way you live, Edith," Zoe had said, with an all-encompassing sweep of her arm around the flat. Whatever Zoe had meant, Edith didn't want terribly to know. Zoe was at best an uncertain reader of others' lives and feelings.

Another acquaintance was a man who saw everything in combative terms. He adored sports, especially American football, and seemed unable to express his thoughts except in sporting metaphors. He had told her she was doing "an end run round the Electra complex." That particular complex she remembered as relating to daughters and fathers, not mothers, but Edith made no comment, for he so enjoyed getting into his sporting talk. "Now, you'd be happier, Edith, if you'd just stop playing shortstop and get in the outfield." Edith wondered what that meant. Was it that she didn't take risks? She hadn't asked.

On that afternoon's walk to Mrs. Dawson's, Edith had stopped before the same shop windows she always did — the lovely little cheese and wine shop, the florist's — coming at last to a corner shop that specialized in embroidered pillows. Edith always lingered before this window. Once or twice she had taken this walk to the tearoom with Zoe and pointed it out. Zoe had seen only the larger picture, the window as a whole, and pronounced it fine. Edith's ability to stand silently and look was annoying to others who wanted to get on with things.

Her mother had often patronized this shop. Mrs. Parenger had done brilliant needlework and had found a compatriot in the little woman who owned the shop. Edith herself embroidered but had never mastered the art. She did, however, have her mother's way of looking. Details, Mrs. Parenger had often said, told the story; it was all in the details; the larger scene would then take care of itself.

Edith leaned closer to the glass. The nuanced colors of the roses in a cushion propped against the leg of a footstool had been expertly done. The colors seemed to be fading right before one's eyes. Her mother was adept at this process of shading and shadowing. *Had* been, Edith told herself, flooded with the sense of loss she had been feeling now for two years. It was ripe pain she was feeling, not old. Tears stung her eyes and she took a deep breath, leaning her forehead to touch the glass. She recovered and looked again at the pillows. Another pillow, done mostly in browns, depicted a whippet and was marvelous in the way the needlework managed to convey the dog's energy. One would really have to get closer, have to pick it up and examine it, in order to separate the patterns, the details from the dark background. *It's all in the details,* Edith heard her mother saying again.

It was only to be expected that such fine attention to detail, such scrutiny, would be brought to bear on other things — brooches and rings, lace and dresses. If there was a flaw, her mother could find it. Edith wished sometimes that she herself couldn't. Still, it was this ability to take in details that allowed her to recognize Archie Marchbanks, when the other customers were simply blind to him. It was that gesture of extending his arm and raising the glasses toward the light that made him irrefutably Archie Marchbanks. He was capable, Edith thought, of putting more into the turn of a wrist than other actors could do with their whole excitable bodies. He had walked away with the otherwise indifferent play. It must have made the leads horribly uncomfortable when they came onstage for their curtain calls to realize the applause had simply spilled over from Archie Marchbanks.

Mrs. Dawson's had been her mother's favorite place for tea because the pastry was so light and flaky and the tea brewed from loose tea, not bags. Edith had finished eating her napoleon and was having a final cup of tea when she noticed him. A slant of sun spreading across his tablecloth acted upon him like stage lighting splashing over the diamond-and-ruby necklace. She had been mesmerized then and was now. . . .

But she could not spend the afternoon here; she would have to go. It took her another quarter of an hour to get her bill from the waitress. She meant simply to pay it, rise, and leave, but on her way to the door she suddenly changed direction and stopped at his table. She seemed unable to help herself. Knowing she was flushing to the roots of her hair, she said, "I'm terribly sorry to bother you, but — you're Archie Marchbanks, aren't you? The actor?" She kept her voice as low as possible so she wouldn't attract attention to him.

He smiled as he nodded.

"I couldn't believe it was you in this place." She looked about her as if she'd surprised them both in some uninhabitable corner of the earth. "You were so good in that play last year."

"Sit down." Archie Marchbanks inclined his head toward the vacant chair.

Edith hesitated, astounded by whatever had propelled her to his table. She was not ordinarily audacious; indeed, she considered herself shy, perhaps the last person to walk up to an actor

150

and tell him how much she'd enjoyed his performance. And she had attracted attention to him. Fortunately, the two at the table next to him had paid their bill and left, but the women at the remaining table had heard her, had looked with curiosity, and had finally realized who this was. They had their heads together, whispering; they were probably plotting out a way to approach him.

"Do sit down," he said to Edith. "You'd be doing me a favor."

She could not believe this, but she sat down.

He was looking around for the waitress. "Would you care for some tea?"

"Oh, no, thank you. I've just had some."

"So have I, but I'm having more. Can we ever get enough tea? I don't think so."

The waitress, a young thing with curls of silky pale hair framing her face, came immediately (although, when waiting on Edith, she had been quite slow and sullen), came wreathed in smiles. Edith doubted the waitress knew who he was; she was probably responding to his youth and exceeding good looks. It was difficult to guess Marchbanks's age, but he could not be more than thirty-one or -two and most likely was even younger. She had, surely, twenty years on him. She was fifty-two. From the waitress came any number of *Yes, sirs, Right away, sirs, I'll see, sirs* before she gave him a little tilting bow and rushed off, her apron starched to within an inch of its life and crackling all the way.

Archie Marchbanks smiled at Edith as if they had both perceived the waitress in the same way. "Do you live around here?"

"Yes, just a few streets away, actually." She named a street off the Fulham Road.

"Oh, yes, I know that street, lovely houses. Not 'purpose built' but 'mansion house.' I love British euphemism."

She smiled. "Mansion houses; you're right. It's very comfortable, our — my — flat. But I expect I'll be moving one of these days."

"Why, if it's comfortable?"

She could hardly bring up her mother's death, so she avoided answering at all and asked him the same question. "Do you live somewhere around here?" Edith didn't really suppose he did; Fulham didn't cater for actors.

"No. Where are you moving to?"

Edith had said she was because it seemed to give her some purpose, to show she was not merely going on with her life but giving it direction. "Oh, I haven't worked that out yet. I've just been looking around." She hadn't; she hoped she had not been caught out in a lie and would therefore have to invent another Edith, living the life this Edith felt she should be living. "Not terribly seriously, though. One hates to move, so much trouble." She was glad the waitress was back to interrupt should he again ask her why, since she was "comfortable."

The waitress had set down the fresh, steaming pot of tea and a cup and saucer for Edith, beamed at Marchbanks, and gone off. Edith did not realize, until she saw her gloves lying on the table, that she'd removed them; nor that she'd slipped her silk scarf from around her neck; nor that she'd shrugged her coat from her shoulders. All of this gave the impression that she meant to stay, that she was making herself at home. She was shocked by this. She simply could not imagine a less likely meeting than this one, or that it would leave her feeling at home. The man she had seen up on the stage a few months ago and herself, an ordinary maiden lady.

"If I do decide, though, it will only be after *The Mousetrap* closes," she said, watching him pour.

He looked up at her, puzzled. "I beg your pardon?"

"The play." It had simply popped out.

"Yes, I know it, but —"

Feeling rather silly, she hurried on. "Decisions I hesitate to make, such as whether or not to move, I tell myself I'll make when *The Mousetrap* closes."

He loved that. He laughed heartily. The women at the rear table, who'd been staring at them — well, at *him* — ever since she'd sat down, were riveted by his laugh. It was the same laugh that had come at several points during his last play. "That's marvelous. What a wonderful yardstick that is. Will it *ever* close? God, how long's it been going?"

"Forty-seven years. Can you believe it? It *will* close, of course; it has to."

"Perhaps. So you're safe for the moment, is that it?"

Edith didn't feel at all safe. But it had rather pleased her, this bargain she'd struck with herself, that significant lines of action or large decisions would be taken only when that play closed. They — she and her mother — had made almost a ritual of going to see it once every two or three years. It was like an amulet, a good-luck piece.

The most important decision was the one about the flat. Would she remain in a place where nearly every object tugged at her, pulled her back, ambushed her? Sentimental nonsense, of course it was, and the best thing she could do for herself would be to take another flat or even a small house and forget the past. This was the advice given by those who did not have to do it. . . .

"I'll put it off as long as I can. I'm not at all good about changing things. I marvel at people who can pull up roots and simply *go*. I've never been good at going." She sipped her fresh cup of tea.

"You probably won't have to. *The Mousetrap* will undoubtedly be there for the rest of our lives."

"Yes, it's an institution, isn't it?" Edith smiled. "Yet I can't think of anyone I know who's actually seen it, except for me and my mother, when she was alive. It must be mainly tourists."

He nodded. "I saw it years ago. I don't think depth of characterization is — was — one of Agatha Christie's strong points."

"No. But that isn't what one goes for, is it? One goes for the trick."

He laughed. "Do we like that? Being tricked?"

"In the context of detective stories, of course."

He picked up a caramel éclair and set it down again. "In that play, doesn't the trick turn on identity?"

"Yes. It —"

"The plot's coming back to me now . . . ah, yes. But it's a very crude approach to the concept of identity, the way she does it. She's not very subtle."

"No, but then she's hardly trying to deal with a philosophical question. It's simply the trick."

He was still holding a section of the paper clamped to his chest as if it were a kind of protective armor. He shrugged. "Anyway, it's always a question of identity, isn't it?" He turned his teaspoon over and over. He had elegant hands.

"It was the question raised in the play you did last year, wasn't it?" It had been such a difficult role, she thought, one that required the actor to give such a layered performance that the audience would be kept suspended between fear and sympathy. Bewitched. She relived the moment in which he held out the diamond-and-ruby necklace, and the absolute lust he felt for these jewels was plain on his face, an expression quickly replaced by a look of polite inquiry as he turned and spoke to the young woman he would almost certainly betray. The reaction of the audience had been almost visceral; she herself had felt as if she were being pulled from her seat.

He had made the poor play nearly a great one; he had certainly turned his own role as second lead into the starring performance. The lead actor was very good but not in a league with Marchbanks. Edith could think of no other role to compare with it — rather, what he had made of it — in terms of absolute villainy, except perhaps Iago.

She told him this. Had it not been so banal, she would have told him the effect was magical, like a magician's effects. What she did say was, "I'm at a loss to see how you did it, how you kept exchanging personas. Or is it personae?"

He smiled brilliantly. "Practice."

She laughed. "Oh, surely not *just*. Not when you could make us all believe in you so much."

Again, he shrugged. "So does a confidence man. It's not so difficult to make people believe in you. You said it yourself: One goes for the trick."

His smile was ambiguous and for a moment, Edith was uncertain. "I didn't mean it quite that way. And we were talking then about *The Mousetrap*."

"Oh, but you wouldn't confine it simply to that play, would you? Anyway, the villain in *The Mousetrap*, was he so different from the one I played?"

"Good God! The difference is astronomical." She brought her hand down firmly on the table, causing the cutlery to clatter and jumping the half-eaten pastries on the plate, and coloring at this display.

He didn't appear to notice. "I'm not talking about the acting, only about the role. Both roles turned on making the theatergoers believe we were one thing and then we turned into another. As I said, it's the trick of the confidence man."

"You *are* oversimplifying. You did not *suddenly* become someone else, as the Christie character did. You slipped in and out of the character. The first time I saw the play I had a difficult time working out whether you were — well, evil or not."

He smiled. "The first time? How many times did you see it?"

"Three. It simply couldn't be absorbed the first time."

He inclined his head slightly, treating it in this spirit, picked up the éclair and took another bite. The cake plate held several bitten-off pastries where he'd sampled them. He said, "I still say it's not much more than a confidence game. We work damned hard at it." He glanced at his watch. "Oh, Lord, I'm late." He called the waitress for the bill. "I've enjoyed this," he said. He was not going to wait for the girl to come and collect. He dumped a little pile of uncounted coins on the table — pounds and fifty-pence pieces — clearly much more than was called for.

Edith wondered if he was this spontaneous, or careless, otherwise in his life. He slung his coat, a pale cashmere, over one shoulder. The day had warmed considerably. Edith gathered her gloves and bag together and they left the tearoom.

Outside, pale sunlight washed over them as he put out his hand and told her how much he'd enjoyed their talk. Perhaps they would meet again. He asked her if she came here often.

She assured him she did, quite regularly every Wednesday and often on Sundays. And sometimes on other days. They parted, but a few steps away he turned and came back. "Listen: as long as we're both at loose ends on Wednesdays —"

She could think of no one less likely to be at a loose end than Archie Marchbanks! But she waited, hardly daring to breathe.

"Why couldn't we have tea together next Wednesday? Here." He inclined his head toward the worn façade of Mrs. Dawson's.

She opened her mouth to reply but astonishment held the words back until she coughed. "I'd love to. The same time, about?"

He nodded, walked off, and turned to wave.

Edith stood staring for a moment. His surprising offer so stunned her that it made her bold enough to improve upon it. "Mr. Marchbanks!" she called. When he stood waiting, she walked up to him and said, "I just wondered. . . . Perhaps you could join me at my flat next Wednesday, and I could return the favor. I mean, I could give *you* tea."

Archie Marchbanks seemed to like the idea and immediately fell in with the plan that he would turn up at her flat the following

Wednesday. It was only the work of a moment for her to jot down the house number. Her flat was the ground floor, she told him.

"Just in case," she said, as she included her telephone number. "One never knows what might happen."

Again they separated, and again he turned to call out to her, "And don't forget our argument!"

"No, no, I shan't!" she called back to him. But the surprise she felt at his clear desire to meet again, and her own boldness, forced the argument (as he had called it) straight out of her mind. Well, she would remember soon enough.

3

Edith retraced her route along the Fulham Road, feeling her step to be jaunty, which was a decided change from the one with which she'd entered the tearoom. Quite deliberately she paused by the several windows she'd stopped at on her way to the tearoom, for she wanted to see them now in this new frame of mind.

As she stopped again at her mother's favorite shop, she thought it was to her credit that she had not dwelt upon her feelings of loneliness and (she had to admit now) desperation. It was safe only now to recognize such feelings, now that the dark well of them had been partially boarded over. Now they could be acknowledged.

Edith rested her forehead gently against the cold glass window of the cushion shop. She felt a painful acceptance of her earlier feelings, the ones she'd carried into Mrs. Dawson's. *Had* she felt that awful? Apparently, she had, or the relief from them would never have been so visceral. Such a physical thing, the earlier feelings, a crippling burden that had now been lifted. Had she remained silent, had she been too timid to approach Archie Marchbanks, it was terrible to think such feelings would still be dragging at her. It was rather horrible to accept this because that cast of mind could easily return to weigh her down again.

But not now, thank God! Her eyes rested on the whippet, sensing its nervous anxiety. The petals around the bowl of roses looked freshly fallen, as if she had glanced away for just a moment and missed their soft descent. That stitches could render such nuances and breathe life into objects was a fresh source of amazement to her. Although she would never have considered it earlier, now she felt she must certainly buy one. It would always be a reminder of her good luck.

The shop was named Timothy's and was owned by a Miss Vole, a nice little woman whose entire life was tied up in her needlework. Her mother and Miss Vole could talk endlessly about embroidery: satin stitches and couching and petit point. Edith remembered a morning that she had left her mother there, talking to Miss Vole. When she had returned an hour and a half later, she had found them in exactly the same spot. They hadn't moved an inch and apparently hadn't considered sitting down.

160

Miss Vole had for many years occupied the flat above the shop when it was an antiques shop. She had supported herself — and quite well — by selling her needlework to a few discerning women (such as Mrs. Parenger) and had occasionally placed a cushion or runner in the antiques shop itself on consignment. Thus when the shop owner decided to sell, Miss Vole thought it was perfect logic that the next step in her life was to buy it and turn it into a shop for embroidered furnishings. She had kept the name, despite no one's knowing who Timothy was.

Edith loved this charted course, this near belief in a life ordained. For when it came right down to the "steps" in Miss Vole's life, she'd found them few and far between. When she was twenty she had taken one enormous step against the wishes of her parents. She had entered a convent.

"I thought it would be calm; it would be quiet, so different from my home life. I wanted only to do my needlework, you see. That was really why I joined in the first place. I had some vague notion that I could put it to work in the convent, you know, making chasubles or prayer cushions. I assumed there would be oceans of free time.

"How naïve I was! There wasn't any free time; they wanted to keep us busy, keep us occupied. And they didn't want us doing what we'd done out in the world beyond the convent. They seemed to be fearful of worldly occupations, of a new person tracking in

the things of this world. So you see" — and Miss Vole spread her hands — *"we were simply at loggerheads. I'd joined because I thought there would be no distractions; I forgot about God."* Here Miss Vole shrugged, as if having made one silly mistake by joining, she was not going to make another silly mistake by staying. And she had left the convent at the end of her novitiate.

Her leaving, Edith bet, was done with the same sweet reason with which she had gone into the convent in the first place. Edith could not help but smile, but she was indeed in awe of Miss Vole. Having had the conviction to fly in the face of her family's objections, she had then had the conviction to stop. Edith (or her mother, or both) had asked Miss Vole if it hadn't been difficult for her to admit she had misjudged the religious life.

Miss Vole had been somewhat surprised at the question. "Why should it?" was her answer. And how Edith had envied what seemed to be Miss Vole's near-perfect freedom, freedom from needing to justify her actions.

If ever anyone had a calling, it was Miss Vole. She was nunlike in her commitment; why hadn't the sisters seen that? Hers was a worshipful nature that surely would please God, despite its not being aimed precisely at Him.

As Edith entered the dim little shop, a buzzer over the door rasped. Miss Vole stepped forth from a rear chamber. After an exchange about the weather, Edith asked to see both cushions in the window, and Miss Vole set about getting them out, stretching across the other displays. She handed them to Edith and stepped back a little, as if she meant to remove herself from Edith's circle of decision. Both pillows were costly — and had every right to be, the amount of work that had gone into them. The whippet was the smaller of the two, but the more expensive. She liked the whippet, and this one projected such nervous energy. But she also liked the muted colors of the roses and loved the softness of the satin quilting. She sighed, shaking her head. (*Edith, Edith, make up your mind!*) Miss Vole's thin and talented fingers were interlaced before her. She looked serenely at the two cushions, telling Edith she had made both. Miss Vole also sold needlework done by others, which, of course, would have to meet her exacting standards. She had told Edith several times that Mrs. Parenger was as good as she herself, especially with drawn threadwork.

Edith said, running her fingers across the needlepoint whippet, "This is quite remarkable. If you hold it even a short distance away, you'd think it a painting. The shading of the browns is quite marvelous."

"Thank you. Yes, I'm fond of my little dog. I'm asking a hundred pounds for that one."

"Too fond to sell it?"

"Ah, well, I'm never *that* fond, am I?"

That was not quite true. Edith had seen regret stamped on Miss Vole's face on several occasions when she parted from her own work. That was her expression now. To Edith the entire transaction seemed a momentous occasion, fitting to the rest of the day's activity.

"I'll have both," said Edith.

TWO

The little flat Edith shared with her mother for nearly twenty years had served for both of them as a refuge. Her mother used to leave her slippers by the door, in order to exchange her shoes for them immediately upon entering. It had been a symbolic farewell to the stress and strain of London living.

Edith's father had died just after she had acquired this flat, with its two bedrooms and spacious living room. It seemed the natural thing for her mother to come to stay. The family house in Putney was not only too large but painful for her mother because everything (*everything, Edith*) reminded her of Edith's father. Mrs. Parenger had at first naturally thought she would carry on in the Putney house; how can one move from a place that has been home for forty-five years? But the wake of Mr. Parenger's death had carried with it a series of small shocks — a cuff link rolling out from beneath a table, a shirt forgotten in the warming cupboard — reminders everywhere of him. It had surprised Mrs. Parenger that she couldn't take it. It was her home; she should live in it until she died. Edith had swiftly cut through all this, insisting that her mother come to live with her. It had been an ideal solution.

The flat was in a mansion house that had been divided into four roomy flats. Edith's was on the ground floor and had the advantage of the garden, which was lovely and quiet. Even with the French window open, there was little to disturb her. And it was wonderful for Barney, her cat. Mrs. Parenger had called the cat Barnard, apportioning to it a dignity the cat did not deserve. How much dignity was there in hiding behind the hydrangeas to hold vigils over the birdbath?

Everything in the flat had been carefully chosen, with an eye not to decoration but to harmony. Occasionally, Edith (and her mother) chose wrongly and there was a misfit to deal with: they spoke of these poor choices in combative terms. The marble washstand *fought* with the granite top of an end table; a side chair *warred* with the wall hanging above it. Thus, they would have to separate the beleaguered pieces. On the other hand, there were odd marriages that turned out quite well: the painted chair that Mrs. Parenger used to do her needlework, pulled out from a gaming table to sit by the light of the long window. Some other delicate piece sitting beside a lumbrous old sideboard — somehow these odd arrangements worked without looking out of place.

The room was beautiful, Edith thought, full of deep chairs and deep colors, many of them garden colors that seemed to absorb warmth in winter and cool shades in summer. It was really the materials, the embroidered surfaces, that pulled the room together. The soft cushions, fireplace screen, needlepoint footstools of wool or linen, all very fine and beautiful, and the best of it, Edith thought, was her mother's own handiwork. Edith picked up a large square pillow from the sofa and studied it. It was the old house in Putney with its gables and gardens, which Mrs. Parenger had done from memory. Because her mother had been unstintingly attentive to the smallest of the small (*Details, Edith*), a shooting star above the Putney house actually seemed to be shooting, leaving its incandescent trail of silver gilt. Gold and silver thread had been used to work the night sky, and a small willow had retained its delicacy through the feather stitching of its dripping leaves. The moon was nearly hidden by a silverish vapor.

She replaced the cushion and got up to wander about the room, looking at the various pillows, runners, and wall hangings. Here was one of her mother's more abstract works: *dream designs* her mother called such pieces. This pillow, titled "The Red Queen," had been done in vibrant, even violent colors and run up in goldwork, shadow quilting, and appliqué. It was dominated by the scarlet figure of the Red Queen. Edith's mother had related a long complex dream about

Alice's toppling into Wonderland; the piece was her rendering of the dream. Edith had never mastered this sort of metal threadwork. Why, Edith wondered, had she never questioned her mother about these dream designs, beyond asking about the technique? They were fiery pieces, swirling, bursting, wild with strong colors.

She came to the French window overlooking the garden. Sitting beside it was a scroll frame on a stand that Mrs. Parenger had got a carpenter friend to build for her so that she could draw it up to the painted chair and work on it. Edith didn't know what it was to be, perhaps another wall hanging. It was a replica of the garden, half finished, and looked painterly. There was the herbaceous border, the willow tree, the birdbath. In the foreground were larkspur and deep blue delphiniums. The stitching was painstaking and dense, with French knots for the centers of the poppies and daisies; the tiny beads on the leaves of the flowers imitated dew or raindrops. The little willow's gracefully trailing branches were done in many shades of silvery-green.

In the kitchen Edith made herself a cup of coffee and drank it sitting at the white enamel kitchen table. She felt heavy, as if she had eaten a large meal and was now suffering its ill effects. The hour with Marchbanks might have been too rich for her, too plentiful and varied for one such as Edith, who was used to less abundant rations. In another moment she was crying. Now it was as if the earlier hours of the day had never happened, as if she'd dreamed the whole thing — the tearoom, Archie Marchbanks, the purchase of the pillows in Timothy's. Indeed, it was precisely the sort of thing one would dream. She did not understand herself. What then had happened to her fine feelings, her exhilaration?

Had she been drifting for many years, half asleep, and now awakened to swift, icy currents? Edith looked at the wall behind the stove where a china plate hung, a whimsical thing better suited to a child's nursery, the story of the owl and the pussycat in their pea-green boat. The boat rolled along on little waves. She had found it in the house in Putney, in the attic she had sometimes explored. The plate had been packed away with other reminders of childhood.

She felt somehow shamed that her life was so narrow, that it covered such a small territory, that if she raised the spyglass she would see nothing but blank gray water. Yet she had always thought she preferred being on her own, except for the company of those now dead and two or three others who had moved away from London. Was this desire for solitude one of the signs of old age? She sat for some moments fingering the linen place mat, refusing to give in to the urge to lie down with a cold cloth over her eyes. That was what she wanted to do, draw the bedroom blinds and lie on the large cool bed. Her bedroom was painted in shades of gray. Edith sighed and wondered what that said about her.

She did not do this; instead, she made another cup of coffee and carried it into the living room. There, she opened the French window wide and pulled the painted chair up to it. The day had grown brighter; now, at nearly six o'clock, the garden seemed to steep itself in all of that collected sunlight, as the birdbath had collected the early morning rain. Her cat, Barney, hid in a camouflaging shrubbery, his yellow lozenge eyes turned toward the birdbath, waiting. She looked at the bright red stock, the foxglove, the blue delphinium, and the pastel shades of the borders and thought she had no reason for discontent. There were too few pristine days like this one; she shouldn't squander them in weeping. What had caused that sudden squall, that little tempest of tears? She shook her head. Yes, it had simply been all too sumptuous an afternoon. Rich, like those pastries Archie Marchbanks had taken bites of. She saw the cake plate in her mind's eye: the éclair oozing its custard filling, the flaky napoleon, the walnut loaf and lemon curd tart. And that irresistible strawberry meringue! How had he managed to take only one bite?

Archie Marchbanks appeared to like everything and nothing. Edith fell to wondering what she could serve him for tea on Wednesday. She could of course simply pick up cakes at Mrs. Dawson's, but she thought it would be nicer to do something herself. Perhaps she could compromise and buy some walnut or orange slices and then make a few Cream Roses.

She told herself that she would not spend every day planning Wednesday's tea.

But of course she would. Although she might try to occupy herself in the flat and the garden, or pay a visit or two to the library or the cinema, these attempts to occupy herself would not be successful in expunging Wednesday's tea from her thoughts.

Already exhausted, she slept. It was all too much, too unreal.

THREE

"How in the world do you do these?" Archie Marchbanks held out his small plate with its Cream Rose as if distance would give him a better understanding of it.

It was with relief that Edith told him. Relief that the week of waiting was done with. It had turned out to be more full of dumb anxiety than pleasant anticipation. All she need do now was pour the tea and pass the cake plate. "The fluting is the only part that takes a bit of practice." Pink and pale and suffused as a blush, they were as perfect as the roses Archie Marchbanks had brought her, and which now stood on the sofa table behind him in Edith's silver Georgian vase.

"You don't mind, do you, if I simply admire it for a bit?"

She said of course she didn't mind. He was sitting on the sofa with the air of an old friend who is certain his presence is welcome.

That Marchbanks had come at all surprised her. Remarkably, there had been no last-minute

172

call, no apologetic change of plan. And until he had stood there in her doorway, she had thought his appearance to be less and less likely. How crowded with engagements, how demanding his life must be! But wasn't that awfully superficial of her, to think it was all applause and adoration?

She was delighted to be offering him some of the walnut bread. "Try this; it's a bit less complicated than the rose."

Archie Marchbanks slid a piece onto his plate and took a bite. "Mrs. Dawson's?"

"Yes, it is. I wouldn't have supposed you'd remember with that medley of pastries on your plate."

"I'm an actor," he said, smiling over the rim of his teacup. "It's my business to remember."

She looked at him blankly, feeling that was somehow an odd answer. She had been about to say this, when he spoke again.

"I think your flat is quite wonderful." He had already spoken his approval of the arrangement of furnishings, the depth of the colors, the "interplay of surfaces."

She had laughed. "You make it sound like a stage set."

Now he was up again, making a circuit of the room. He stopped before the French window, open on another pale blue and gold afternoon. Even the weather seemed to be cooperating with their tea party. With his back to her, shaking his head, he said, "So this is what you intend to give up" — now he turned and smiled — "when *The Mousetrap* closes?"

She flushed and looked away. She wished she hadn't told him about that harmless game she and her mother had played; it now seemed such a foolish thing to admit to. Why had she told him? Her voice steady, she answered, "That wasn't exactly what I said. I would *decide* what I'd do then. It's making decisions that I find difficult."

He had moved to where the painted chair half hid the scroll frame holding her mother's embroidery. He knelt down, studied it, picked it up, and took it over to the window. "Beautiful. It's your garden?"

"Yes."

He returned the frame to its place against the wall and took his seat again on the sofa. "Why on earth would you leave a flat that seems so perfect in every way? That has your imprint all over it?"

"My mother's imprint, you mean. Most of the embroidered pieces are hers. She was very good." She poured more tea. "That's quite a disapproving frown you're giving me. You'd stay, I expect."

"Go on living here? Of course."

"Even if a place is too full of memories?"

He raised his eyebrows. "Surely, that's all the more reason to keep it." He picked up his cup. "Are the memories painful?"

"Memories are generally painful." She surprised herself with this quick answer. Picking up the blue glass plate holding her Cream Rose (which she, just as he, hadn't yet eaten), she laid her fork beside it, saying, "I mean simply that they're painful by virtue of that part of your life's being over — that day, that year; you know." She disliked the turn the conservation was taking. With such a visitor as he, the talk should be absolutely heady, not, for God's sake, the same business she brooded over daily. She steered it onto a less dangerous course. "You told me to remember the argument. About *The Mousetrap*." For some reason, she hated to disturb the Cream Rose. It was as if, once she split it with her fork, it too would become one of those memories. How absurd. Deliberately, she took a bite. It was a lovely, smooth confection of meringue, whipped cream, and strawberry mousse.

"Cleverly concealed identity, wasn't it? I read the play again, incidentally."

"Really?" Edith was pleasantly surprised to find the earlier conversation had made such an impression on him.

"The villain was perfectly believable. He was plausible. The audience has no reason at all to question his role."

"Only I wish the others wouldn't go to such pains to *appear* guilty."

Marchbanks waved this comment away somewhat impatiently. "That's not the play; that's the acting and directing."

"I'm not sure what point you're making."

"That it's all a confidence game, surely." He smiled, got up, and shoved his hands deep into his pockets as if that aided his thinking. "For example, I expect I have your complete confidence."

She laughed. "That depends what the confidence is *in*."

"That I am what I say I am. That I'm Archie Marchbanks."

"Oh, dear." Edith gave an exaggerated sigh. "Or that *I*" — she smiled, she hoped, wickedly — "am Edith Parenger. And as such, I still fail to see your point."

He shrugged. "That nothing really exists outside of its role."

"This is sophistry." It amazed her how easily they fell into argument, as easily as others fell in love. She smiled. "Please, let's not have one of those tiresome arguments about the nature of reality. No one really lives by them, anyway."

"Lives by them?"

"Those arguments. I mean, that whatever 'reality' is or isn't, we still get up in the morning and drink our tea." She picked up the teapot as if by way of demonstration. It was cold.

"You don't question it?"

"Well, of course I question it. But not as some philosophical system. If I'm hurt in some way, or terribly ill, I might say *Why me?*" Edith amazed herself. She was, ordinarily, reticent, though not because she lacked conviction. "Right now, I think we should have more tea." She held the pot aloft.

Marchbanks laughed.

But she didn't rise. She said, "You know, I'd much rather hear about your life — or what

176

passes for your life — since the way you question reality tells me you don't appear to know if you're living it."

That made him laugh again. "My past?"

"Assuming you've had one." She was being, perhaps a little too arch.

"Oh, you've made your point. Now, what about the tea?"

Edith took the cold teapot into the kitchen. Marchbanks trailed after her, stopping in the doorway. She ran water into the dented electric kettle, feeling a little embarrassed over its condition. Really, she should get a new one. "I'd rather hear about the present, actually. What's this play you're doing?"

"It's the new David Crael one."

Edith brought the tea canister down hard on the counter. "I knew it! The one everyone's been speculating about." David Crael had not produced a great body of work, only three plays in his fifteen-year career. He was thought to be more lucid — at least superficially lucid — than Pinter or Stoppard, the writers with whom he was often compared.

Archie laughed. "Oh, I imagine there might be someone or other who doesn't give a damn."

"I read somewhere — was it in an interview? — that he wasn't going to stage it because he couldn't find the right person for the lead."

Marchbanks smiled. "He must have found him, then." He pressed one hand to his heart. "Archer, *c'est moi.*"

She turned from measuring out the tea, puzzled.

"Oh, you know. Flaubert and Emma. *Emma, c'est moi.*"

She smiled. "Yes, I know Emma. But who's Archer?" She put hot water in the teapot, poured it out.

"That's the name of the character, my character. It's rather a small cast."

"And do you really become your character? As Flaubert claimed to have become Emma?"

He watched her spoon the tea into the pot. "Aren't we in danger of falling into another discussion of reality?"

Edith filled the teapot with hot water and said, "Is that what I'm talking about? I don't think so. Let's go back to the other room."

Seated again, she said, "You still haven't touched your Cream Rose."

"No. It's too perfect. Like the elegant little figures one sees made of marzipan."

She asked him again. "*Do* actors become the characters they play? I really wonder."

He shrugged. "They say they do. Perhaps they do. I don't."

"*You* don't? Given your last role, I would think you must. You were so terribly into it."

Marchbanks laughed as he broke off a bit of walnut loaf. "I would hope I was into it. I'm an actor, after all."

"Then . . . if you don't become your character, what *are* you?"

He raised his eyebrows. "Calculating."

Edith shook her head. "You can be quite exasperating sometimes."

2

Exasperating, yes. But she was perfectly happy in the way the friendship was going on. For the last several weeks, they had met every Wednesday, sometimes at Edith's flat, sometimes in Mrs. Dawson's, where Marchbanks continued to take bites out of everything on the cake plate. Anyone would have taken them for old friends. Edith felt they were. In Mrs. Dawson's, Edith could not help but enjoy the reflected glory of it all. He had either got used to it or he honestly did not notice the sensation he caused. The ladies (more and more of them) were expending a lot of energy in trying *not* to notice him.

On this particular Wednesday, Marchbanks studied one of Mrs. Dawson's lemon curd tarts and returned it to his plate. He had been explaining the lengths the playwright David Crael would go to to keep his new work secret. "It's why I'm in South Ken during the week. For rehearsals. David refuses to have them in a theater, so he's rented a lock-up."

Edith laughed in disbelief. "Rehearsing in a lock-up garage in South Ken? You are joking, surely?"

He shook his head. "No, it's the truth." When she opened her mouth to reply, he held up his hand. "If you're going to ask which garage, don't. You already know more than anyone else in the world outside of the cast and crew. But I feel you're one of the rare people who can be trusted."

Edith merely nodded, but she was terrifically pleased.

"He's doing his own directing, David is. To tell the truth I think he'd have preferred to do it *all* himself — lighting, set design, costumes, acting; there are only four of us in the cast, so he might just have managed — and sell tickets to boot."

Edith laughed again. "And, no doubt, write the reviews."

"David doesn't bother about reviews. He's one of those lofty artists who shuns the opinions of others."

"It doesn't sound like it; otherwise why would he be going to such pains to keep the play secret?"

Marchbanks shook his head. "It's not because he fears criticism. I think it's because he feels it *is* a secret — you know, the way some artists and writers have to keep hold of their work until it's done."

"Yes, but this play is —"

"Done? No, not for David. We have yet to see the ending."

"What?" Edith gave a little gasp of surprise. "He's going into rehearsals with an unfinished play? I don't understand."

Marchbanks turned his smile from her in the direction of a heavyset woman with papery light-brown curls, heading for the table. She flushed so deeply Edith was afraid the poor woman would have a stroke; her hand, when she held out a paper for Archie to autograph, trembled. He signed it, handed it back with a smile. Hurriedly, she returned to her seat.

It had not taken long for word to spread, after their second visit to Mrs. Dawson's, that Archie Marchbanks was by way of being a regular. Mrs. Dawson (wherever the dear lady was) had increased her business, yet the customers took some care to avoid staring at him, and only three or four times had one nerved herself to approach him. Had he been a film star, it would have been impossible because of that larger-than-life impression film people can't help but make. Edith had suggested that they could, after all, meet in her flat on Wednesdays, every Wednesday. But, no. Assiduously, Archie had insisted on taking Edith to tea at least once in a while, and he thought Mrs. Dawson's probably the most private, or at least the most respecting of privacy, of any establishment they might find.

So here they were, at the end of June, a month after they had met. "I don't understand," Edith said again.

"Oh, the end is finished; he's written it, of course. He simply doesn't want *us* to know about it until he can no longer hold out." Marchbanks crumbled some of his square of shortbread, frowning slightly. "You know, come to think of it, it could very well have been a part of his reason for wanting us, especially Nell —"

"Are you talking about Nell Tuitt?" He nodded. "How *lucky* for you!"

The thin smile he gave her suggested that the luck might well be Nell Tuitt's. "Anyway, as I was saying, the other two" — he named two actors who weren't well known — "they don't even come into it until nearly the end; but Nell and I — David might have chosen us because we don't mind —" He paused. "We don't mind hanging by a thread. At any rate, David wasn't going to take a chance on some critic or reporter stealing a march on opening night."

The opening of a new play was always public long before it opened. A David Crael play — well, that was an event. He hadn't done one for nearly seven years, which appeared to be the pace of his writing. He was not prolific.

"Anyway, Nell doesn't seem to mind; neither do I, not if that's what he wants."

"You're both showing a good deal of forbearance, I think." Edith sipped her tea. "I think she's simply — wonderful!" She felt she was gushing, which was something she seldom resorted to. But she did think Nell Tuitt was wonderful. The actress had a reputation for being extremely modest, with none of the self-serving *artistic sensibility* that Edith imagined too many actors were cursed with. And with all of her fame and money, it was awesome to Edith that Nell Tuitt lived quietly with a husband, a cat, a dog, and two teenage children near Clapham Common. Interviews had told her that much, and the pictures that accompanied them showed a woman with a serene expression, a comfortable face. "I recall in one interview she said she had no wish to be glamorized. She said, 'I'm a better victim.' I always thought that interesting. Is she?"

Marchbanks was motioning for the bill and getting change out of his pocket. "Victim in David's play, you mean?" He was thoughtful. "I expect so."

"Don't you know?"

He smiled. "Remember, we don't have the ending yet."

The waitress with the brown curls came quickly with the bill. She seemed to regard their table — and it was so designated ("Oh, yes, sir, I've kept your table for you") — as her particular property.

Edith laughed. "You do make it sound as if the thing's just being written as you go along."

He looked at the bill, put down far more than the total. "You know, I think that's just what David wants. At the beginning he said he wanted us to think our way through the script."

"Oh, for heaven's sake," said Edith, with a dismissive little wave of her hand. "The actors might as well play charades."

"You think it's all empty talk?"

"Well, don't *you?*" When he didn't answer, she went on. "I suppose I shouldn't be making judgments on such a little bit of evidence. It's one of my faults. But as far as the ending is concerned, you know, it's rather fascinating. Not to know, I mean. Still, you must have some idea; there must be clues."

Marchbanks was ironic. "Like *The Mousetrap,* you mean?"

"No, of course that's not at all what I mean." She was impatient. "We're not talking about the clues one finds in mysteries."

"Is there that much of a difference?" He smiled as he reached around for his coat. The sunlight had turned to drizzle and would no doubt turn back again. "Clues. I'll have to think about it."

3

Their meetings continued for some weeks, well into the summer, as long as he was engaged in these rehearsals in this undisclosed garage in South Kensington. They talked a great deal about the theater, Edith trying to guess where these clandestine rehearsals were held, Archie not giving her even the whiff of a clue.

They talked — or, rather, Edith talked — about her family. Edith spoke at great length about her parents, especially her mother; about her sister, whom she rarely saw. "We just never got on, that's all." There was the old house in Putney, which had been too big and — her mother had said — too haunted. Her mother had sold it.

"There you go again," he said. "Selling up memories."

Marchbanks said little about his own family.

Edith didn't know if he had any siblings or if his parents were still living. But he was like that; he talked a great deal, but a lot of it was abstract argument or hypothetical question. Somehow, Marchbanks was elusive. She could not pin him down.

"I can't imagine," Marchbanks said on this particular Wednesday, as his eyes moved round the room, "giving this up." His fingers traced the raised stitches on one of her mother's pillows.

Edith said to him, "I know. I expect I can't either." While she had fretted about giving up the flat before, now she was less inclined to do so.

"This is fine, this pillow." He held the embroidered side so that Edith could see it, as if she might not be familiar with all of the pillows.

She smiled. "Yes, it is. It's what's called bargello work."

He raised his eyebrows.

"You have to find your pattern. You find that medallion shape by sliding mirrors across the charted background. The mirrors have to be at right angles to one another."

Marchbanks looked again at the needlework, frowning. "What a complicated process. I don't see how it works."

She smiled. "But it's simple; half the medallion is a mirror image of the other half."

He shook his head. "Not simple to me. Your mother must have taken her needlework seriously."

Edith thought that sounded a trifle patronizing — as if on such pursuits a serious cast of mind was wasted — but she said nothing except to offer him more tea.

"Yes. Thanks," he said, as he took back his cup.

He appeared to be restless. He rose from the sofa and walked over to the French window, rested his hand on the back of the painted Italian chair.

"Is something the matter?"

"What?" He turned. "No, nothing." He left the window for the wallful of books. He pulled out one in a worn leather binding and thumbed through it. "John Webster. *The Duchess of Malfi.* I'd give anything to play Ferdinand." Suddenly, he snapped the book shut:

"My sister, O my sister, there's the cause on it.

Whether it be from fortune love or lust

Like diamonds we are cut with our own dust."

Edith was amazed. Marchbanks's swift and violent transformation into the frantic Ferdinand left her breathless.

He retrieved the copper-colored book and returned it to its place. "Great stuff."

"Never tell me again that you don't become your characters. I've just seen you do it. Are you going still to claim what you just did was calculated?"

"Of course it was. You don't have much contemporary stuff, do you?"

Edith smiled slightly. "If you mean by that, I don't have any David Crael, you're right."

Marchbanks turned. "You don't like his plays?"

"Oh . . . I didn't mean that." Although she hadn't much liked the man's last play. It lacked passion to the point of seeming heartless. And the creeping progress of this new play made her think she'd like it even less. It sounded artificial and egotistic. But of course Archie Marchbanks, being the wizard that he was, would probably turn it into gold. What Edith said was, "That last one of his that I saw, it seemed a bit cold, I thought."

Finished with the books, Marchbanks came back and slid down on the sofa. "So is this one. Like a block of ice. Fortunately, it can be melted and moved. By me." A mock smile flashed and disappeared.

"And Nell Tuitt?" Edith asked, smiling also.

4

Edith's friend Zoe called several days later to discuss their luncheon date the following week. It was always the third Wednesday of every other month, and it could be that Edith had entirely forgotten because the dating of these luncheons was so complicated. Had the luncheon occurred once *every* month, the date might stick better. Now it had been some seven or eight weeks since

187

the last one. Edith felt as though she hadn't seen Zoe in years.

Edith apologized, said she couldn't make it on Wednesday, and couldn't they change it to Thursday? Or perhaps Tuesday? Of course not, Zoe had said, and reminded Edith that Thursdays were always her gallery days (Royal Academy, National Portrait, Tate) and Tuesdays were shopping days (Harrods, Liberty's, Upper Sloane Street).

Edith had known before she suggested it that the Wednesday date couldn't be changed, not because it was important but because Zoe's days were so completely booked. Zoe's week was tightly, even stubbornly planned, and inflexible. There was no room for maneuvering. Overturning one appointment would, as far as Zoe was concerned, bring down the whole house of cards. Which was what she told Edith over the telephone: "If I start swapping dates there'll be no end to it."

Zoe had her life planned into the foreseeable future. All else was havoc. Edith had once seen her filled-in calendar, and it was quite daunting. She put Edith in mind of a perfectly trained circus performer, judging the moment the trapeze would swing to her fingertips with uncanny accuracy, executing her turns and spins in defiance of gravity. Zoe was always on time, but always in a rush because (Edith suspected) rushing reinforced the illusion that she was accomplishing things. Zoe was not, Edith suspected, aware of any of this, but was compelled by it — the full calendar, the spot-on meetings, the dates set in cement.

"It's always been Wednesdays," Zoe said again. "Before we settled on a definite date, our lunches were all helter-skelter. It didn't work at all. You remember." What Edith remembered was a more relaxed luncheon. Zoe went on. "It simply throws me off, throws off my entire day, my whole *week*, you know that!"

"I'm terribly sorry, Zoe." And Edith was, hearing that edge of panic in her friend's voice. She was sorry enough that she revealed at least part of what made the Wednesday lunch impossible. "I ran into someone — well, someone rather unusual — and Wednesday is the only time he has free." She realized of course as soon as she said it that she'd never get off so lightly.

"Honestly, Edith! It's the only time I have —" Zoe stopped, as curiosity took over, curiosity being stronger than Zoe's need to remonstrate. "Who? Who's unusual?"

Edith hesitated. She did not want to tell Zoe, or anyone else, really. She felt like a child blessed with an enormous secret that sharing would somehow squander. And she smiled. Perhaps she could understand David Crael's feeling about his new play. She said, "It's an old friend. You don't know him."

"No, and I didn't know you had an 'old friend.' I've known you fifteen years, Edith. How much of an older friend is this person?"

189

"I don't mean old in that sense. It's merely someone I knew before under entirely different circumstances —" Oh, what abstract nonsense she was talking!

"I don't know what you're talking about. What's his name? You said *he*."

One thing no one could accuse Zoe of was scattered attention. Zoe heard every word and remembered it. Edith sighed, resigned to speaking the truth. "Marchbanks. Archie Marchbanks."

"I don't recall you ever mentioning any Marchbanks."

"Zoe, I *know* I didn't. I haven't seen him in years."

"Well."

Nothing else? Just *well?* To Edith's astonishment, she realized that Zoe didn't recognize the name, at least in this context. It seemed impossible, but there it was. Yet, Edith recalled that Zoe didn't often go "up West" to the theaters; indeed, Edith thought the last show she might have seen was *Cats.* Or perhaps *Les Miserables.* Musicals, that was what Zoe liked.

"But surely you're not tied up with this person every Wednesday *forever?*"

"No, of course not, but it would make things much easier, wouldn't it, if we could work out something else. . . . How about dinner on Wednesday instead of lunch?"

"Dinner. . . ." Zoe murmured this in a way that suggested she was turning it over carefully, as if it were an eccentric but not unpleasant notion.

It was the days that Zoe so carefully con-
structed. Nights had never presented much of a
problem. Edith couldn't recall anything Zoe did
with her nights, other than *Cats*. How odd. It was
generally the coming on of darkness that made
most people anxious, wasn't it? Perhaps nights
were taken up by her family, her husband and two
children — when they were home from university
— none of whom appeared to occupy Zoe's day-
time thoughts. Rarely did she speak of them, and
only when she was irritated because one or another had interfered with Zoe's scheduled luncheons, museums, galleries, shopping. The
daughter's name was — Gemma? Was that it?
The son's Edith couldn't recall. Zoe's husband
was Harry. A thin, pale man who did something
in the City. They all seemed to be perfectly satis-
factory, but perhaps that was because they hadn't
made much of an inroad on Zoe's consciousness.

"Well, all right. Yes, dinner might be quite all
right. I'll just have Mrs. Sipp do something
about dinner here."

Who was Mrs. Sipp? wondered Edith, but she
didn't ask. Mrs. Sipp apparently didn't stand very
high up in the previously engaged hierarchy if she
was so easily available. Edith named an hour for
meeting, to which Zoe agreed, and rang off.

5

"You know, there are times I think of giving it up."

It was the Wednesday after the dinner with
Zoe had been accomplished when Marchbanks

made this surprising disclosure. They were sitting at their usual table in Mrs. Dawson's.

Edith glanced up from her teacup, frowning. Since he couldn't be talking about the meringue swan he held, he could only be talking about David Crael's play. "But don't you have a contract?"

Puzzled, he was looking at the complicated little meringue, as if it had been engineered to keep him guessing. But the look was for Edith. "Oh, you mean David's play? No, no. I mean acting altogether." He took a bite of meringue, returned the damaged swan to the cake plate.

She could not believe he meant that. Arguments rose thick in Edith's mind, but she was too staggered to formulate them. She felt as if she'd literally taken a blow to her chest, got the wind knocked out of her. For once she saw the aptness of that old cliché. "But . . . you can't, that's all. You're one of the best — certainly, at this point, *the* best-known actor in London."

He flushed, as if embarrassed by his own celebrity. He picked up a cream horn. Bleakly he smiled. "I expect that's it, you know. I'm not set up for that sort of thing."

"From what I've seen, you're quite brilliantly set up; you handle fame amazingly well." Her tone was ironic as she gestured toward the tearoom's women customers.

"I'm . . . I think I'd like an ordinary life." He paused as if inspecting his words for their aptness. "I want" — he looked at her, smiling — "to be anonymous."

Edith hardly knew what to make of this. "Like me, you mean?" Her arm moved in a small arc that circumscribed the tearoom. "Like us?"

"Something like that." He bit into the cream horn, looked thoughtful. "What I really want to be is someone like an accountant: you know, a dreary job that fed me but that allowed me to go back to my flat and simply have a meal and watch the telly."

Edith was truly impatient. "Oh, for heaven's sake. You only say that because you aren't an accountant."

"Then I don't want to be admired quite so much. I might enjoy being a shop assistant, someone like that."

"You can be so tiresome at times, Archie. I can't really believe you. No matter what your natural talent, you'd have to have worked tremendously hard to get where you are. What you're saying sounds so — disingenuous. You'd rather be a mediocre shop assistant than a gifted actor, is that it?"

Marchbanks smiled wryly. "No. I'd rather be a *gifted* shop assistant. After all, I have my pride."

They both started laughing. They spoke of it no more.

C

As he was scooping thick Devon cream onto his scone, Archie said, "I'm afraid we'll have to suspend our meetings. The play's opening a week from Tuesday."

Edith just looked at him. Finally, she managed to say, "You mean the preview performances?" The air in Mrs. Dawson's, normally warm and redolent with spices, suddenly had a chill in it.

"Preview?" Archie laughed.

Edith failed to see the joke, but then she was at the moment not especially in the mood for one. She really did not know what to make of this announcement, doubly difficult for their having their tea today in the tearoom, where it was not easy to retreat. At home she could simply have made an excuse to go into the kitchen. But not here.

"Can you imagine David 'trying out' this play? What I told him was, we should go directly from opening night to closing. Which would give precious few people precious little time to work it all out. The play could then remain his secret." Archie laughed again.

This might have amused her had he not preceded his comments about David Crael and his play with the fact that they would have to *suspend* their meetings. It was difficult not to give in to the temptation to ask him exactly how many weeks did he mean? How many Wednesdays? Or to suggest another day, any day; she was quite free. Archie's remark was all the worse for his seemingly easy acceptance of the Wednesdays he would miss. Edith felt cold; her hands were freezing. She put them in her lap, rubbed them together. It was as if these afternoons meant little to him, really. She could say nothing of all this but tried to match his airy manner by saying, "Well, isn't that a shame? The play opens a week from Tuesday? Then you could perhaps come to the flat next week?" Her voice at the end of these questions almost betrayed the underlying intensity of the need which made her ask them. When he said, yes, of course next week, her relief made her light-headed.

"Our Wednesdays would be difficult; you see that." He bit into a lemon square, studied it as he chewed, returned the rest to the pastry plate. "Wednesdays are matinee day for this play."

Edith gave a little start, a rush of pleasure, for he might be going to suggest another day. "Then you mean . . . another day, perhaps? Well, I think I could manage —"

With a vagueness that made her uncomfortable, he said, "We'll see."

We'll see. Was that all he had to offer? That banal and patronizing bit of comfort? But she told herself to be reasonable. He could hardly be in Fulham having tea and giving his matinee performance as well. So it didn't mean he didn't care about their meeting. Except . . . his expression was so awfully sanguine. She looked quickly away, looked at any other object or person but him, at anything else in the tearoom, anything else but at his comfortable and languishing figure. Turned slightly sideways, legs jutting out before him, ankles crossed, he gave the impression of being so at home, one might wonder that he would prefer any other place to

195

Mrs. Dawson's Tearoom.

Her breath came more easily. Had he not intended to keep up their little tea parties, he would hardly have said, "We'll see." She bent her head, forced herself to continue eating the strawberry tart. That she could take any comfort in such an unpromising phrase as *We'll see* only served to tell her how far gone she was.

1

When he arrived at her flat the following Wednesday, he seemed dispirited. That was quite all right with Edith; he should, she felt, be a little sorry. Edith had gone to some trouble, had made a seed cake and a tart and got some very good strawberries at the greengrocer's.

She wasn't surprised when he reverted to the subject of their Wednesdays. It was as though he thought he might not have made it clear to her the week before. The demands of the play, he said. Although she wasn't surprised, she heard all this with a sinking heart. She had not until now felt how ephemeral the relationship was, how easily dispensed with. But "ephemeral" wasn't really the word. "Unrooted," perhaps. Or rooted only in imagination. She began to think of their meeting places — her flat, the tearoom — purely as stage sets. A divided stage, perhaps, one set illuminated, the other pitch dark. And then the reverse, light-dark, dark-light. Back and forth.

"I'm so sorry we won't be able to do Wednesdays anymore. What a delicious tart this is!"

We won't. As if half the responsibility were hers. She murmured a response, but her thoughts were taken up with what he'd said. *To do* Wednesdays. He really *might* have been that shop assistant he claimed he felt such a kinship for. *Yes, madam, we do scarves; yes, we do gloves.*

So this was to be their last tea together for some time. Realizing this, Edith felt a hollowness that bordered on terror. It was not so much that their routine would have to be changed (to the point even of there being no routine at all), but that the prospect didn't appear to bother Archie Marchbanks. Her tone was deliberately sardonic when she asked him, "And do you like the ending?" She said this to his back, for he had risen after returning his bitten tart to his plate.

Now Marchbanks was standing in the French window looking out at what he called the "unsullied" garden. Nothing stirred in it, not even the oat-colored cat, crouched and unmoving as a piece of garden statuary. "I don't know," he said.

Edith found she was capable of even more surprise, of renewed interest: *"What?* Oh, but surely —!"*

He turned, a faint smile on his lips. "No, it's the truth. David's letting us in on it tonight. You see, it doesn't require any of us to *do* anything. I mean, there are no new lines to be learned. No new turns to take, expressions to devise, meanings to explore —"

To Edith, it sounded as if he were talking to

himself. "Even *so*, there'll be things for the audience to discover."

"Yes, but not for us, not for the actors." He started back to his seat on the sofa.

"There must be clues scattered along the way."

"Yes, I suppose there are." Sitting, he scraped his hair back in a boyish gesture. "If one is paying attention."

Edith lifted her cup from its saucer but set it down again quickly, as she couldn't stop the tremor in her hand. "I should imagine anyone who's having to pay thirty quid for a seat is certainly going to be paying attention." She tried to stop the landslide of her feelings by making reasonable, even chilly replies.

But it was as if she hadn't spoken. He carried on with his thought. "Because otherwise, if one didn't anticipate the ending, one might find their situation — intolerable."

"By 'their' I assume you mean the characters' situation?"

He nodded, rose again, nervously. "If the ending's what I think, then it's rather — vicious."

Edith looked up at him. "Then why are you smiling about it? Is it so clever?"

"Yes." Marchbanks laughed. "Perhaps that's the point at which the audience comes into it."

"I have no idea what you mean." Her tone was measured and cold. It was one of those rare moments when she felt herself to be absolutely right. Let him explain himself, dear

God! She wanted to weep.

He didn't. "It's the surprise; I think he wants us to be surprised."

Feeling in the midst of her sorrow something like contempt, she rose and said, "This is ridiculous. Are you sure there is such a play?"

It was his turn to be surprised. "Good Lord, Edith, do you think I've been fabricating all of this?"

She looked into the dregs of her teacup. "What you say the director is doing doesn't make any sense. The actors' surprise will be over after tonight, but the play will run for at least a year. How will he wring three hundred and sixty-four more nights of surprise from you?"

"Yes." He sat back. "It sounds absurd, I agree."

This infuriated her. He could hand over the absurdity of it to the playwright. She knew her tone was hopelessly sarcastic. "Aren't you going to offer to send me a ticket?"

He looked at her, and his look was somewhat sad. "I don't think you'd like it, frankly."

Which was such an unexpected answer even she had to laugh.

Marchbanks left a few minutes later. At the door to her flat he said, "We'll have to resume these tea parties in the future."

"When *The Mousetrap* closes, you mean?" Her face, a mask, refused to soften.

He laughed. "I hope we shan't have to wait

that long. . . . I've really enjoyed our Wednesdays, Edith," he said, somewhat more solemnly. "I'm sorry."

But neither his voice nor his face was apologetic. She was sunk; she was unable to match his breezy manner and was a little surprised when Marchbanks bent his head and kissed her on the cheek. She took no comfort from this; it seemed merely the last detail in the pattern. She stood in her doorway, a stiff smile on her face, watching him go out the front door. When he started to turn, probably to wave, she quickly retreated, not wanting to be thought of as wringing the last morsel from their meeting.

She went back to the living room to collect the tea things. The cups and saucers clattered against the pot. It was perhaps a bit too showy, the silver tea service. Edith returned the tray to the piecrust table and sat down in the painted chair, still in its position by the French window. She picked up the scroll frame leaning against the wall and rested it in her lap as she looked out over the garden. It was always a little shocking to find that after a huge upheaval in the mind or heart everything outside oneself remained exactly the same. The hydrangeas were as deeply colored as ever, the cat still lay in wait in the shrubbery, a robin twitched on the edge of the birdbath, and from a distance she could hear the bells of the Brompton Oratory.

I don't think you'd like it. The words took on a more sinister tone when she was left, on her own, to turn them over. What Marchbanks had said was really immensely patronizing — no, worse; it was cruel. Surely he could not believe for a moment that she would not want to see this play. The point wasn't whether she liked the play; it would make no difference if she loathed it. It was Marchbanks whom she would be going to see. And far from discouraging her, it would have been more natural, surely, to tell her he'd send her a ticket or leave one at the box office.

Edith sighed and looked down at her mother's tapestry. Perhaps she had been right, her mother, in attempting these complex arrangements, for such work was demanding and one had to stay focused. *When it gets down to the truly complicated part* (her mother had said), *don't think you can talk and stitch at the same time.*

FOUR

There were days to be filled as there had been before Archie Marchbanks. Edith had been with him for only a few hours a week, yet it seemed so much more, for there had been the preparation and anticipation leading up to those Wednesdays and the pleasant musings leading away from them. In this way, her week was largely occupied with Marchbanks.

Now Edith wondered what in God's name had occupied her time *before* Archie Marchbanks. She did not remember her days as having been barren and empty; there surely had been a pattern to them. For Edith knew how much she was a creature of habit, enjoying the same things — Mrs. Dawson's, the cushion shop, the excellent cheese shop, and her cup of tea and a book before going to sleep. These were all the raised parts of a pattern she had established, those parts to which the eye was drawn; the muted backdrop was of those places and people she did not regularly see, and because of this were allowed to seep back into the ambiguous background. They were not parts of her ritual, as were the lunches with Zoe (now restored to their original Wednesdays). There were visits with Miss Vole; day trips on the train to places like Brighton or Stratford; the Tate Gallery and the Victoria and Albert.

Perhaps she was not much different from Zoe with respect to how she spent her time. No, that was not the case. Edith didn't have a schedule; she could easily switch from one thing to another on one day or another. Had Edith been seeing a psychiatrist (as was Zoe), she would of course have to keep to a fixed time. And he would become part of the pattern that stood out in bold relief. She actually contemplated starting therapy, one of the milder forms — not the exhaustive treatment Zoe was engaged in, certainly. But she honestly could not think what she had to tell him. Or her. A woman might be more helpful, given the loss of her mother (though instinct told her the sex of the doctor was probably irrelevant); in Zoe's case it was clear to Edith that her friend was responding to her male doctor as if he were her mother, which, unfortunately, was not clear to Zoe. Edith thought it might have helped Zoe had she been aware of this. For Zoe, the causes of her unhappiness had begun in the nursery; Zoe was always making fresh discoveries about herself and drawing unlikely (Edith thought) conclusions. This did not make Edith suspicious of psychiatry, only of Zoe.

But Edith herself? What complex relationships

had she that would require a doctor to unravel them? She could think of none. If Edith was miserable, she was perfectly aware of the source of it. And she sincerely doubted a secret life of the mind was going on beneath her awareness — of her mother's death, of Marchbanks's behavior — that denoted yet another pattern, one of long-standing misery.

The days, the days. It was nearly a week after her last tea with Archie Marchbanks that found Edith sitting in the painted chair that now seemed permanently placed to look out over the garden. She had picked up her mother's embroidery of the garden scene and was running her finger over the gold and green stitching. Needlework was at least one thing to be taken up again. She set aside the scroll frame and went in search of her own piece, barely touched in these last weeks. Her mother's work was far better than her own. Edith hadn't the deep attachment to color and line that made her mother a virtual Impressionist, a kind of pointillist in thread. Her mother, like Miss Vole, had been devout in her practice of embroidering. Edith again recalled the two of them standing in the cushion shop talking about drawn threadwork: how when she had gone back after over an hour, they were still talking about it, standing where Edith had left them. It was as if there were literally nothing else in the world except drawn threadwork, nothing worth their regard. Good heavens, Miss Vole had even wanted an environment in which no one was permitted to *talk* and was willing to join a convent to get it.

Edith hadn't this cast of mind, clearly. This was the deeper difference between them. She was much too analytical. Even if she hadn't Zoe's problems waiting to ambush her around every corner, she still considered herself to be fairly deep. It was this analytical turn of mind that made her sensitive to what was sham or shallow — which was why she disliked David Crael's work. Yet she certainly gave him credit for raising sham to extraordinarily high levels, so that it almost turned the corner into honesty. He had very little to say, but was masterly in saying it. But was that possible, really? He was an enigma. Were these thoughts about David Crael simply holding at bay similar thoughts about Archie Marchbanks?

Edith had been sitting by the open French window for a long time, long enough for day to turn to dusk. She looked down at her piece of embroidery of a starry night and wondered what had moved her to attempt such a difficult piece of needlework. The pillared house, lights at the windows, and that sky, all done in petit point and Gobelin stitches. Ordinarily she did surface embroidery. She liked to experiment with wavy lines and metal threads, like Japanned gold, that got its effect on the cheap. That made her smile slightly; it was rather what she had thought about David Crael's plays. Or perhaps it was what she was attempting *not* to think about Archie Marchbanks.

There had been no mention of the play's week of preview performances because there had been none. If David Crael had been as successful as she supposed in keeping his play a secret, its listing in the theater section would not have appeared before today, Tuesday. It was difficult to believe that the play could appear with no advance publicity, but it had. She had seen no mention of it in either of the daily papers she read. The play would appear like a genie out of a bottle to astonish reviewers and the theatergoing public alike. She could be cynical and say this was just David Crael's trick to generate even more publicity. But somehow she didn't think so; she believed what Marchbanks had told her about Crael's wanting to keep the play secret. Edith saw in his work a love of secrecy. It could even be that opaque quality that, in the end, made his work inaccessible for most people.

She put aside the hoop filled with the starry night and went to the kitchen to retrieve the paper, which she had used to cover the counter to collect flower trimmings. She swept these aside and found the entertainment section, which she took back to her seat by the window. There was still enough light to read by, with her glasses. Yes, here it was: "A new play by David Crael." It was called *Elsewhere*, the sort of title that invites ambiguities of time and place, just the sort she would expect David Crael to come up with. In larger print there was ARCHIE MARCHBANKS and NELL TUITT. It had opened today, as he had said it would. Matinee, Wednesdays; two performances on Saturdays. Edith tore this announcement from the theater listing so that she would have the telephone number. She should call right now, but she knew the box office telephone would be busy for a long time. Better to call in the morning, as soon as the box office opened.

Or perhaps she was being precipitate; perhaps he had every intention of seeing she got a ticket, probably several extras for friends. Perhaps he was even planning on a theater party and would invite her. Perhaps, perhaps. . . .

She lowered her head, resting it on her palm, and looked out over the garden where, in a sudden shaft of light, the old crumbling statue blazed whitely and two robins perched on the cement bath. She wondered if the cat was still in its hiding place; she had not seen it move.

Edith sighed. *I don't think you'd like it, Edith.* No, there would be no tickets waiting at the box office. How she wished she'd kept quiet about *The Mousetrap* and her childish way of using it as a hedge against change. She should have kept that back, even if she kept back little else. And really, she thought, within the confines of good taste she *had* kept back little else. Why couldn't she have handled the relationship with the facile touch that he himself had brought to it? For Marchbanks (she realized now) was a canny conversationalist, one of those who made listening such a fine art that one had the impression he was himself doing most of the talking. Archie Marchbanks had been in quest of — what? Nothing, she supposed, but an opportunity to while away a few tedious afternoons that would put him to no trouble.

She felt exposed, onstage herself, with all those eyes taking her in. Her face was hot. But white-hot. Glowing, perhaps, like the statue with its blind eyes.

FIVE

When Zoe found out about the play, and that Edith had a ticket for the Thursday night, she asked why Edith hadn't got two tickets, that Edith surely must know how much she was dying to see it. Edith told her she didn't know; Zoe seldom went to the theater. And anyway, there weren't two tickets together to be had, not even for the matinee. Now, if Zoe would be willing to sit in another part of the theater by herself . . . ?

Naturally, Zoe said of course she didn't want to sit by herself. Zoe wouldn't. Zoe was one of those women who simply couldn't go out into society by herself, couldn't eat in restaurants alone, go to plays or films. Galleries, yes, but there everyone was more or less by himself, wandering about looking at his own private paintings and sculptures.

Edith knew she'd refuse. It would no doubt have been possible to get two tickets on this Thursday since she'd called a week ago. But certainly not two tickets as good as her single one. Her seat was on the aisle and in the fourteenth row, a plum. And she hadn't wanted anyone with her when she saw it for the first time. She was sure that she would see it more than once, and as the weeks went by, tickets would be a little easier to come by. Perhaps she would treat Zoe. Zoe was the sort of person to whom one was always making amends, even though one was blameless.

Thursday night came and Edith found herself in the lobby, crushed between a woman in a fig-ure-hugging black jersey and another who had splashed on too much of a heavy, earthy scent. They were the companions of men in rather vio-lently colored waistcoats, all of them talking about David Crael and his oeuvre. The woman in black actually said this. Edith had never before heard the word spoken but was sure the woman was mispronouncing it. The four were great ad-mirers, but Edith doubted David Crael would have wanted to be around them, around anyone who spoke of his oeuvre, or perhaps anyone who spoke of him at all. Edith smiled, recalling Archie Marchbanks's comments about secrecy.

This made her fonder of David Crael (and his oeuvre — not a very large one, since this was only his fourth production) than she otherwise would have been. She believed that even if his play was impenetrable, he himself was deadly se-rious about it. One could depend upon him not to hoodwink his audience intentionally.

The buzzer sounded for the first act, and Edith was more or less carried along by the people on all sides of her. She wondered briefly if anyone had ever been trampled to death by a theater crowd; not only was it heavy in the lobby, but there were all those people on the pavement pushing from the rear. When she finally got to her seat, she was thankful it was on an aisle, for she could stretch her legs for a moment.

The lights dimmed, people coughed, programs rustled, and breaths (it seemed) were suspended. The audience seemed aware that this was the theatrical event of the year without being told so by the reviewers. Reviews always colored her reaction to a play, so she was just as glad she hadn't seen any.

The curtain rose slowly to show a corner of a public park with synthetically green grass and glossily leaved trees, evenly lit in bright sunlight. None of this green and gold was so overt it was distracting, but it seemed heavily symbolic in its suggestion of fakery. Edith observed how the yew hedge at the back of the stage was pruned to topiary perfection in the fleur-de-lis pattern across its top, a perfect design carved out of tiny leaves. The primulas and petunias were so very neat, they looked painted there. And that sky! Such a blue as Edith had never seen — so deeply, falsely blue. All in all, the set struck her as stylized and unreal. Edith liked elaborate sets; streetlamps throwing disks of light into swirling fogs of Victorian drama, or the gilt and velvet of some overinvolved Restoration comedy. Even an inferior work could be almost (not quite, though) redeemed by the mazy details of a complex set.

There was plenty of time to consider the set, to make up one's mind as to whether or not one liked it; Edith disliked it intensely. It made her uncomfortable for herself and uncomfortable for the actors. It offered no support to them. No soft cushions to fall back on. They must flail as best they could; and this was, perhaps, the play's point. She had wondered after seeing Crael's last play if he hated his own characters and thought that, yes, he very well might. Edith squinted at the program, looking for scene changes. There wasn't one until the third act, and there only in the third scene. So she would have to look at this pinched and glaring little park for nearly the whole of the evening.

Along the gently curving path that ran by a dry concrete fountain were three iron benches. Nell Tuitt (Julia, in the play) sat on one, reading a book. Archie Marchbanks (Neil Archer) sat across from her on the other side of the path, reading a news-paper and eating a sandwich. All that one could hear for a full two minutes was the rasping sound of the newspaper and the pages of the book being turned. It was startling how long a minute could last, thought Edith. It seemed forever, which was one of the Crael effects — to make time stand still or speed up. The silence here created a great deal of tension.

The action began when Julia looked across the top of her book at the man on the other bench and frowned. The frown gave way to surprise (pleasant, apparently) when she looked at the back of her book's jacket and then across again at the man. It was evident that he must be the face on the back of the book. For several moments after putting the book in her lap she seemed about to speak. Finally she did — delight, timidity, awe all registering in her tone. Yes, she had correctly identified him; yes, he was Neil Archer. When it was certain she had before her the famous novelist and she tried to talk, her tongue sounded swollen in her mouth, stumbling over words that she felt needed saying, expressions of admiration and gratitude for his marvelous books. It was clear from her fluttering movements and her halting speech that Julia was aware of sounding banal, and that she wasn't at all banal, she was intelligent and insightful. It was marvelous the way Nell Tuitt conveyed this because her actual lines, her words, sounded flat and platitudinous.

Archer for his part was easygoing and affable. But, of course, he was the object of all of this admiration. Marchbanks's beautiful voice sounded deeply sincere. Neil Archer was rich, he was popular, he was well regarded by the critics, and he was a simple man. After all, wasn't he eating his lunch here on a park bench?

"Care for one?" he asked Julia, holding up the brown bag. "It's cheese salad — like the old joke about the fellow who hated cheese salad —"

"What old joke?"

"Oh, you know. Man complained over and over about always finding cheese salad in his

213

lunch box" — Archer was unwrapping a sandwich — "and when his mate asks him why didn't he make his own, he says, *I do.*" He raised his face to stare at the blue sky. "Somehow that joke lost something in my translation."

Julia laughed. "Yes, I have heard that joke."

Archer said, "I wonder if it might not represent the ultimate in controlling a situation."

"Or having several pounds of cheese salad at home."

Edith smiled. She liked Julia, a person with a practical turn of mind. And she liked Nell Tuitt's ability to project so much empathy.

The conversation continued in this way, a great deal of it the ordinary (or seemingly so) discourse one might expect from an acquaintanceship struck up by two strangers. It appeared they had much in common, but of course (Edith knew) they hadn't anything in common. David Crael wouldn't allow them to have. She felt a swift sadness move over her, lightly, quickly, as if a breeze had ruffled her hair.

No, they had nothing in common. Edith was troubled by this.

There were two intermissions, unusual these days. At the end of the first act, the applause was (as to be expected) resounding. It was almost a relief to get away from the formidable tension conveyed by these two actors, get away and go out and have a cigarette on the pavement or a drink at the bar.

Edith had had the foresight to order her gin and tonic before the first act and now found it on a corner table with a slip of paper bearing her name. Her mouth was dry; she was thirsty from the excitement of seeing Archie onstage. She smiled, though, looking around the crowded room, thick with talk and brandy and nearly blue with smoke, and wondered what everyone would say if they knew the lone woman standing in this corner had met Archie Marchbanks in much the same way that Julia had met Neil Archer, and would — just as Edith and Archie had — probably go on meeting him.

And even with that realization Edith hadn't seen it coming.

It was not until halfway through the second act that it all became chillingly familiar. Up to that point she had only registered the connection between Archie onstage and Archie in her flat. It wasn't until Neil Archer said to Julia, "I'm thinking of packing it in; I'm thinking of quitting," that Edith stiffened in her chair, her hands grasping the arms of her seat.

"Oh, no. Oh, you mustn't," Julia wailed.

"I'd simply like to be anonymous for a change. Sometimes I think I'd like to be a shop assistant. To go home at the end of the day and watch the telly."

Julia sympathized; Julia understood. Archer's thirst for anonymity was much like others' thirst for celebrity. There was always the hunger to be someone else, wasn't there?

Edith wanted to bolt. But something pinned her down. She had the fanciful notion that everyone in the audience would guess if she suddenly left. That all of these eyes fastened on Neil Archer would turn to fasten upon her. What kept her in her seat was resolution; she would not be turned out of it. Resolution and no small measure of healthy curiosity. She kept watching the two actors with a kind of fascinated horror. How far would he go? How far, with her, had he *gone?*

"I like to climb aboard a double-decker," Neil Archer went on, "and just go where it takes me. A purposeless ride. I like being a face in a crowd. But if such a character as that were to be put in a play or a book — well, it would defeat the purpose, wouldn't it? Or, I should say, the pur*poselessness.* In the end, art lies, doesn't it?"

Around Edith, Marchbanks had stopped just short of expressing such pretentious sentiments. For had it been Edith sitting on that bench across from him, she would have said, "What nonsense" or "Don't be tiresome." But that did not make the similarity between the two situations any less striking. He had not expressed such sentiments because he had not been encouraged to do so. The analytical side of Edith's mind was still working in spite of the extremity of her feelings. And that side wondered how David Crael could put such sham ideas into Neil Archer's mouth. But perhaps that was the whole point. It was so easy for Julia to be taken in. Julia begged Archer to reconsider, begged

216

him not to give up. There was a great deal more said about art, Archer suggesting that they might be, the two of them, "characters in some hack writer's novel."

After a silence, Julia said, "Oh, but we're not."

That was the end of the second act. Grateful that she had the aisle seat, Edith was not greatly disturbed by people crawling over her to get to the bar. Only the couple sitting beside her wedged past; the others in the row went in the opposite direction.

She still sat. Her face burned; her entire body burned. The beginning of the third act she suspected she could predict, but not the end of it. She simply had to see how it came out, had to see what David Crael would make of it.

Their next meeting in the park had Archer looking chagrined as he said, "I won't be seeing you for a while; I have one of those promotional tours to do, the ten-cities-in-a-week sort of thing. You know how that is."

It took Julia some time to answer. "No, I don't expect I do." Her disappointment was palpable.

The program read TEN DAYS LATER. This was the second scene of the third act: Julia, seated on the same bench, her purse clasped tightly in her lap. There is nothing she can say; there is no one to say it to. The tour was to last a week; the week was over. Edith glanced at the profiles across the aisle from her, the faces bathed mysteriously in the theater's lambent light. She wondered what they thought and if they understood that Neil

Archer was not going to return. And would they understand why? Edith didn't. Not at all.

The final scene was the one in which the set changed. The curtain came down but the lights did not come up. There was a deep, dense silence in the theater. The curtain rose upon Julia, standing in a bookshop before a display of new fiction. This was a huge pyramid of one title, Archer's latest. And here were the other two players, a shop assistant and a customer. Julia took a book from the pyramid, opened it eagerly.

Edith knew, with a shock, what this scene would do and how the play would end.

Julia had opened the book and read a bit, picked another section, read a bit more. And more. It was quite amazing that even from the distance of the fourteenth row — and probably all the way to the rear of the theater — one could see the transformation of Nell Tuitt's face. Edith thought she could see even the shifts of expression on Nell Tuitt's face with the growing realization she had been used. And the awful thing about it was not that he'd written his and Julia's meeting into a book, but that he'd written the book before they met. Archer had written their script.

The set then expanded into a dazzling arrangement of mirrors, in which the figure of Julia was reflected into infinity. It was quite a display of pyrotechnics, but Edith wondered if this symbolism was even necessary; she wondered if the point hadn't been made already by Julia (with

the help of Nell Tuitt) herself. In the background were signs of weather that never came —
reverberations of thunder, reflections of light-
ning, echoes of rain.

Edith left as the curtain was coming down,
again glad she was sitting on the aisle. She did
not want to stay to hear the applause. As she was
getting her coat and leaving a pound for the coat-
check girl, the applause continued. She still
heard it echoing as she walked out of the theater
into a rain that fell like glass rods. She could even
hear the applause beneath the rain hammering
the pavement, or imagined she could.

2

Edith sat in the painted chair at midnight,
drinking warm milk heavily laced with brandy
and looking out over the dark garden.

What had Marchbanks been doing?

He could not write lines already written by
David Crael, so if the play had already been
written, what good was she as an experiment?
What in God's name had Marchbanks hoped to
experience? Had he thought up this charade
from the moment she'd approached his table in
Mrs. Dawson's Tearoom? Had he perhaps
wanted to see how convincing he would be in the
role? Had he wanted to see if it "worked?" Surely
not. Archie Marchbanks knew he would be convincing; he didn't have to practice on an un-
known woman.

Unlike Julia, Edith hadn't responded to him in

a way he would have found useful. He couldn't get at what he needed, and she assumed that he needed what Archer needed of Julia. But what was that, exactly? Edith did not know what he wanted; and neither would Julia have, but Julia at least had spoken her lines marvelously well; her response to Neil Archer was assuringly predictable.

Edith's own lines weren't comfortably predictable. Whatever Marchbanks himself had been looking for, it was certainly not common sense; he wasn't looking for Edith's "I don't believe you."

To judge by this play, common sense was the last thing anyone was looking for. And she was fairly certain it would sink beneath the weight of its ambiguities and, perhaps, its pretentious solipsism. It would last only as long as Archie Marchbanks was there to keep it afloat. (And Nell Tuitt, let's not forget *her,* dear God.) Archie would want to go on to something new. Actors usually did.

3

A year later proved Edith right. She could not help but follow theater news in the Arts section of her paper. Archie Marchbanks was in rehearsal for another play, not a play of the caliber of David Crael's but a play he would drag by the scruff of its neck toward success.

She had given up *The Mousetrap.* That game she had played with herself had no appeal for her anymore. It had been a secret between Edith and Mrs. Parenger, and the secret having been told had tainted it. But she continued her Wednesday visits to Mrs. Dawson's, sometimes going on Sunday too. It made her uneasy to realize the number of times she mistook someone else for Marchbanks, for his looks were certainly not in common circulation: someone just darting onto a District Line train in South Ken, or reading the paper in a restaurant window as she passed, or turning a corner on St. Martin's Lane. For Edith couldn't help but go into the West End when she wanted to see some production or other and, going, would sometimes pass the theater where Archie's new play was in rehearsal. The high black letters of his name up on the marquee were larger than the name of the play.

Looking at the big posters, at the photographs of Archie Marchbanks, she couldn't help but wonder how it all might have turned out if she'd read her lines right, if she'd been a better actress. She hadn't been good enough; she hadn't been Julia. She never saw him again.